Magic, Mischief & Mayhem

A collection of magical works

S.N.Arly

Copyright

Magic, Mischief & Mayhem: A collection of magical works

ISBN: 978-0-9913209-1-2

Cover designed by Neal Rasmussen.

Acknowledgments

Writing when you have a family is rarely a solo endeavor, so I would first like to thank my awesome husband Steve for making sure I get some writing time, and my children Beren and Ranna who have done an amazing job understanding that sometimes mommy needs to play with her words.

I wouldn't be the writer I am today without the encouragement and constructive feedback from other writers. To the members of Guts and Rocks, past and present (Kelly McCullough, Anne Waltz, Stephanie Zvan, Katie Ferreira, Dana Baird and Katya Reiman), and the members of Pengames (Hilary Moon Murphy, Katya Reimann, Beth Hynes-Ciernia, Linda Lounsbury, and Qat Orkin Oskow), I greatly appreciate the time you took to give me honest and useful critiques, even when I turned in strange experimental things. I am grateful to Celia Badon who sent me my very first acceptance letter, and who bought the story "Dragon Tale" twice because she liked it so much. Thanks, also, to Eric Heideman, editor of Tales of the Unanticipated, for his feedback on many stories, and for providing me opportunities to appear in his anthologies and to get over my fear of public speaking through readings and convention programming. I would also like to thank Neal Rasmussen for the absolutely beautiful cover and the title (which fits better than anything I came up with).

Table of Contents

A Gift of Sky

"Do you want to play with us?" Rellin asked, his voice gentle and slow, as if he thought Shya might not be able to understand him. An eager wind pulled at the long white fringe dangling from his coat sleeves and pants, fanning it out behind him.

Though she would have loved to join the other children, she shook her head and looked away from the pity on his face. The branches below her were full and lush, and only a few patches of ground were visible through the gaps when the boughs danced with the weather.

"Leave her alone, Rellin," Bexa chastised, her blonde curls bouncing in a playful breeze. She was Shya's sister and protector, although all her siblings watched out for her. It was utterly humiliating that Shya's staunchest defender was two full years younger. "You know she doesn't fly well."

Shya turned her back on them, in part so she wouldn't hear the rest of the conversation, but also so she wouldn't have to see them soar easily into the sky, where a group of children waited. Unlike the birds, sky folk didn't need wings to fly.

1

She made slow but steady progress along the wide branch, toward the three-level tree house where she'd been born. It was a cool day, which meant she wouldn't be able to save herself if she fell, but she'd lived all of her thirteen years with the same danger. She had fallen out of trees more than once, and still, she liked heights. If she could fly, she wouldn't be afraid of going up higher than the birds did. *If* she could fly.

"Shya Skychild, *what* are you doing out there?" a woman demanded, her voice issuing through an open kitchen window. "Come in here this instant."

Shya sighed as she felt gentle breezes nudging her toward the door. "I'm coming." If her mother had her way, Shya would never leave the safety of the house. The door blew open before she could reach for the handle. She took her time hanging her coat on its peg, hoping she might be able to sneak through the kitchen without a reprimand. Her soft leather boots made no sound as she crossed the hardwood floor, and for a moment she thought she might make it.

"What were you doing out there?" her mother asked, stopping her in her tracks. "You know better than to go out onto the big branch alone."

"But mummie, I'm always careful," Shya insisted, turning toward her mother. "And the big branch doesn't sway or move like some of the others, so it's not *that* dangerous."

Her mother frowned. "We've been through this before, darling." She walked over and caught her daughter's face in both hands. "You aren't strong enough to be out in this weather." Her fingers absently tucked stray strands of straight blonde hair behind Shya's ears. Because she couldn't control the winds, and they rarely obliged her, her hair tangled and knotted if it grew too long. So, unlike any of her kin or clan, she wore it very short. "Why don't you go up to your room, and I'll bring you some nice hot tea."

Shya sighed again and nodded. She wished they wouldn't treat her as though she were sick. It was almost worse than those who assumed she was simple. She had pale pink skin while other sky folk wore a tan. She supposed it made her look unwell in comparison, but it was just that she spent so much time inside, or

2

under the canopy of trees. She was as tall as others her age, and she surely wasn't wasting away.

She knew full well what was wrong with her. She'd heard the healers explain it to her parents, and it was shared in whispers throughout the village. Her third spirit was weak, and always had been. She didn't *feel* weak, but there was no other explanation. The third spirit was summoned during a child's naming, and it brought the magic of the folk. Shya hardly had any magic. She could barely float, much less fly, and then only on the warmest summer days when the sun was hottest. She couldn't call a breeze, and even the elders who had lost their ability to walk or climb could ride the wind.

She walked through the great room to the stairs that circled the great tree trunk at the center of the house. A hand rail had been added when she was about six, but she refused to use it. She didn't care how anxious it made her parents. She hated living like an invalid. Besides, how was she to get stronger if she didn't push herself?

So far it hadn't seemed to make a difference.

The only good fortune to come from her ailment was the privacy of her very own room. Reading had been deemed a safe activity, one of few, and Shya had turned her room into a library of sorts. She had the largest collection of scrolls in the village. Papa had built yet another shelf to hold the inevitable new additions she would acquire in time. Sky folk were superstitious about the treatment of the afflicted and insane, so neighbors often brought her scrolls when they came back from their journeys, though they didn't give souvenirs to anyone else.

Off to one side of her desk, she had two scrolls half unwound and gently held down with flat wooden placeholders. The rest had been carefully set on the shelves in their proper order. Shaman Westwind's sole lesson for her had nothing to do with magic, unlike the other children, and everything to do with the care and arrangement of her collection. Dust wasn't permitted to settle on Shya's shelves, though she had to get rid of it the slow way with a cloth.

She would have liked to be helpful. Her siblings all had

3

positions of some sort, with responsibility commensurate with their age and temperament. Shya's lack of magical potential inspired a lack of confidence in her general abilities. No one wanted her taking care of their children, as she'd once done. To keep the little ones within her reach, she'd made harnesses attached to long leads. Their parents had been horrified. Children had to be allowed to fly freely, they'd insisted. She wasn't even trusted to herd the sheep, and that was a ground bound activity... most of the time. The neighbors had argued that she'd be unable to retrieve strays or fight off predators. Some worried her frailty might attract wolves.

Instead, Shya collected scrolls. She read. And she dreamed of finding a cure that would make her a proper sky folk.

* * *

"Nana Tern dreamed the world, and so it came to be." The tale wasn't new, but the audience was spellbound. The woman had a way with words, and a power even Shya could feel. It was no wonder she was the fire folk's clan shaman. "She built the mountains and filled the oceans. She conjured fire and sky. All this, she gave to the people she had created. But the people did not understand these gifts. They tumbled off the mountains and drowned in the oceans. They were burned by the fire and feared what the sky could bring."

The woman stood and slowly looked at the sky and fire folk seated around the fire. Her dark brown eyes appeared black in the low light, and the reflected flames glinted like eerie orange pupils. Her gray-streaked, black hair was back in two braids. Sky folk preferred loose flowing styles and never bound their hair. Shya was certain the woman met her eyes, pausing, before she continued around the circle.

"So from the people, Nana Tern gathered up four folk to be the stewards of her gifts." The woman smiled, showing bright white teeth in a red-brown face. "The mountain folk know the caves and the peaks. They found power in stones and the dirt of the earth." She flung out her right hand, opening it toward the center of the circle. A handful of dusty soil spread out in a brief puff over the fire for just a moment, and the crowd gasped in amazement.

4

"The water folk know the rivers and oceans," the woman continued. The familiar tale had become more exciting, with anticipation of what tricks she might next employ. "They found their power in the liquid that gives us all life." Her left-hand came out, and a gentle spray of water sprinkled out into the flames, making the wood sizzle and crackle. "The sky folk, who know the heavens, found power in the winds and weather." She pursed her lips and let out a slow strong breath. She rolled her head at the last-second, and a gentle breeze wrapped around the fire, making the flames twist in an unnatural spiral. The sky folk applauded and cheered in delight, though it wasn't the end of the story.

When the crowd quieted, the woman continued. "The folk of fire know the way of flame, and find their power in heat and all that burns." She held out both hands and the flames rose to twice their height. They suddenly curved at the tip and dove into the woman's hands. Shya gasped along with the other sky folk, then stared, utterly captivated. She had never seen fire magic so close. The shaman glowed orange and yellow, but the fire dancing on her skin didn't hurt her. She turned her palms back toward the empty fire pit, and the flames returned to their place. "Each of these folk were set the task of teaching others to understand Nana Tern's gifts, while also protecting the world and its many wonders, including those which seem frightening."

After the story, Shya stayed seated while the sky and fire folk stood and began to mingle. The air was filled with greetings and introductions, too many to follow. While she had seen some of the other folk occasionally, this was the largest group to stop by her village on a trading journey. Nearly fifty fire folk had arrived in their wagons that afternoon. They fascinated her, but she was too shy to talk to them. She was afraid they might think she was bad luck, as a clan of water folk had believed. She'd been unable to participate in the festivities during their visit, a year ago, and had to settle for watching it all from the trees, where she couldn't be seen. If she was careful, the fire folk wouldn't notice her, and she wouldn't be sent away.

"I don't blame you for keeping out of the crowd," a woman said, her low voice sympathetic.

Startled, Shya turned to see the storyteller sitting beside her.

The woman smiled. She had crows' feet at the corners of her eyes, and thin lines around her mouth, but Shya couldn't have guessed her age. "I'm called Kell. What's your name?"

Surprised that someone so powerful and important would bother speaking with her, Shya stared for a moment before realizing she was being rude. "I'm Shya. Shya Skychild." She had to say something to keep the woman from asking about her magic, something polite. "Your story... I've never heard it like that before. It was amazing."

Kell chuckled. "It was all showmanship and simple tricks."

"I didn't just mean the magic," Shya said. "You made pictures in my head. I saw the ocean. I think I could even *smell* it."

"Well thank you." Kell inclined her head slightly. Up close, she was only a little taller than Shya, but she'd seemed *huge* when she was telling the story. "Do you like tales?"

Shya nodded. "I collect them."

Kell looked intrigued. "Do you?"

"I have scrolls from all over the land." She caught her lower lip in her teeth, wondering if it might have been better to keep that to herself. Would Kell think it odd that a thirteen-year-old collected scrolls? Would she want to know why?

"I have a collection of tales, as well," Kell said. "I can't bring them all when I travel, but I have a fair few along." The sound of drums carried through the gathering, tentative and without a steady beat. That would change. "Would you like to see them?"

Shya was stunned. Not only was the fire shaman paying attention to her, she'd been invited to see the woman's scrolls. Shaman Westwind hadn't let her near his. "Oh, I couldn't," Shya said, wishing she didn't have to politely decline something she desperately wanted. "I'm sure there are others who must want to speak with you, and I couldn't impose."

Kell grinned, her mischievous expression making her look no older than Shya's sixteen-year-old sister. "I'm not one for crowds, so I'd thank you for imposing. And if it makes you feel better, we'll make a trade. You can show me your scrolls tomorrow."

"You'd really want to see them?" Had she left her shelves tidy and ordered?

Kell stood up. "No one will miss us."

Shya followed the older woman into the shadows surrounding the two straight lines of wooden wagons. Oxen, horses, and mules were picketed down both sides of a wide aisle between. When sky folk went trading, they flew and carried only what they had to. Their trips rarely took them far away. Water folk preferred the rivers, and traveled by foot within a few miles of their landings. Mountain folk roamed everywhere in small groups and slept under the open sky, in small tents, or caves when they could be found. Fire folk journeyed great distances, using elaborate wagons as traveling homes and shops.

"Where do you live?" Shya asked.

"We have homes of wood and plaster," Kell explained. "Our clan hails from the foothills of the mountains to the west."

The mountains couldn't be seen from the forest, but Shya had heard of them. "That's far away."

Kell nodded, the movement almost invisible in the dark. "And we'll go farther before turning back." They walked side by side. "Here." She held out her hand, directing Shya toward one of the wagons. "Not all of us have come, of course. Someone has to stay behind to keep the home forges burning. And not everyone enjoys the road."

Metal steps were mounted on the back of the wagon, leading up to a small door. Shya's parents and older siblings would have had to duck to make it through. She stepped into the wagon and froze. It was so dark she couldn't distinguish shapes, though she could hear her hostess moving ahead of her. A pale white glow started up, further in. It was tiny and useless at first, little better than a spark, but it slowly grew into a proper flame.

"I'm sorry," Kell said. "I don't want to blind you, but it's much too dark in here for either of us to appreciate my treasures." After a moment, she lit a second candle.

Shya looked around in awe. She'd never seen the inside of a wagon, and it was marvelous. Just past the door along one wall was a bunk bed. Cupboards with secure looking latches lined the opposite side. The wood had been stained a dark red brown color, and the hardware, hinges, hooks and knobs, were all gleaming brass, a reminder of the fire folk's skill with metalwork. A table was mounted to the wall below a small window, just beyond the bed.

Kell opened one of the large cupboards and waved Shya over. "These are the ones I can't leave home without."

Shya's eyes grew round. The shelves were close together, so the scrolls weren't stacked on each other. The paper on every one was tightly wound, half around each of the two wooden dowels that bound them. The connected rolls were held closed with wide ribbons, the color indicating the scroll's subject matter. White ribbons were for stories and tales, dark green denoted agriculture, and light green was for healing. Black, which bound none of Shya's collection, marked the scrolls pertaining to magic. Kell's scrolls had been divided into two sections, roughly equal in volume, white and black.

Kell reached in and pulled out a scroll of tales. "This is one of my favorites," she said. "I've had it for nearly a decade, and I still take it when I travel." The edges were worn, and the paper discolored. It was long, and Shya wondered if it was a single story or a collection of several. The woman of fire gestured toward the table. "You could read for a while if you like."

Shya looked at the scroll, then strained her ears for the sounds of the gathering outside. Would anyone really miss her so soon? If her parents noticed her absence, they probably assumed she'd gone home to bed. They thought her more frail than she was, and she often stayed up to read long after they sent her to sleep.

"The party is only getting started," Kell assured her. "But I'd understand if you want to go back to the dancing and music."

Shya shook her head. "I like music."

"But not dancing?" Kell asked with a laugh. She shook her head. "Your interests run much like my own."

Shya sat down and carefully removed the white ties, laying

them flat on the table beside her. She gently rolled the scroll, winding more paper onto the right dowel as she made her way to the beginning. She was unfamiliar with the tale, which detailed how Nana Tern selected the folk from the people. It explained how the three spirits worked together to maintain life. The first, arriving on conception, got things started, but couldn't support a life alone. The second came at birth and taught the body to breathe and eat. The first and second spirits had to be compatible. Disagreements between them could cause illness or even death.

She immersed herself in the words, reading well past the point where her eyes were dry and tired. She was oblivious to the sounds of others returning to their wagons as the party wound down. Before she reached the section on the third spirit, the section that might prove most useful to her, she had to set the scroll aside. She lay her arm on the table and rested her forehead near her elbow. Her mind was abuzz with information, so she didn't think she'd ever fall asleep, and she meant only to rest her eyes.

* * *

Shya woke to strange sounds and even stranger smells. People were talking, some were running, and she could hear the laughter of children. That was wrong. Her bedroom window opened to the trees, and sky folk *didn't* run. Her head throbbed, and her eyes felt full of sand. When she opened them at last, she looked up at a ceiling she didn't recognize. She started, rolling to her left, and fell out of the top bunk of a bed with a yelp.

"Are you all right?" a woman asked, her voice concerned.

Shya had landed on her hands and knees, and the shock traveled up her arms to her shoulders. Wincing, she sat back on her heels, looking toward the front of Kell's wagon. She recognized where she was, but couldn't imagine why she was still there. "I think so." She tried to remember what happened before she'd fallen asleep, but her headache made thinking difficult. She felt like she'd stayed up all night reading, and realized she had. She shook out her arms, quickly assessing her actual injury. Nothing felt broken, and she'd had enough broken bones to know. Her knees would bruise in another day, and her wrists felt sprained, both of them, though mildly. The pain was deep and sharp, but only when she moved wrong.

Kell helped her up, making her sit on the lower bunk of the bed she'd just fallen out of. "Here, let me take a look." She checked Shya's hands first, then ran her own over the wrists. She frowned. "These are going to hurt, and I'm afraid there's nothing I can do about that."

"It's okay," Shya said. "I'm used to it."

Kell looked puzzled, but didn't ask. "I'm so sorry. I thought you'd be more comfortable higher up." She stood. "And I didn't think sky folk could fall like the rest of us."

Shya looked down at her bare feet, embarrassed.

"Now what have I said to upset you?" Kell asked.

"I'm not bad luck, really, I'm not," Shya said quietly. "I'd *know* if I were."

"Who said anything about bad luck?"

Shya didn't answer for a moment. "I have a weak third spirit," she finally said, furious with it for ruining her life. Her eyes stung, and she knew that wasn't a holdover from her late night of reading. She took a deep breath, angry with herself for almost crying in front of someone she barely knew. She glared at her hostess. "I'm not good at anything."

Kell's expression softened, but didn't change to one of pity, which was just as well. Shya would have run out of the wagon then and there, without her boots, if she had to endure that on top of her other humiliation. "I very much doubt that you're not good at *anything*," the older woman said. "Now come to the table. You should break your fast."

Shya got up and found that a bowl of warm oat mash awaited her. A plate of early raspberries was in the middle of the table. "Thank you," she said, feeling awkward as she sat on the bench. "I'm sorry I was rude." What would her parents think? Her parents... "I should get home," she said urgently, standing up.

Kell shook her head. "Sit down and eat. Your family knows where you are."

The oat mash had been sweetened with something that wasn't maple sugar, but it was good. There was also a little cinnamon, which Shya was familiar with. She ate in silence, still embarrassed and unsure what to say. Her wrists twinged a reminder when she moved them, so she made an effort to keep them straight. It was difficult, and she'd need to bind them soon.

Kell sat down at the other side of the table. "You don't look like you have a weak third spirit," she said after some time.

Shya glanced up from the bowl. "I can only do the teeniest magic."

"Would you tell me a little more about the magic you *can* do, and what you're supposed to be able to, but can't?" Kell asked. "I'm not trying to hurt your feelings, I'm just curious how your magic works."

How her magic worked. Shya let out a snort. Strangely, it didn't hurt to be asked, when asked the right way. "Sky magic uses the winds." She shook her head. "But I can't speak the language. I can't make the winds understand me, and I don't know their words."

Kell nodded. "That makes sense, in a way." Resting her elbows on the table she leaned forward, looking at Shya as though trying to see under her skin. "Fire magic is much the same, as I imagine all magics of the folk are. The flames have a language, and in order to command them you have to be able to speak it." She leaned back and shrugged. "Some of us have a greater vocabulary, but all fire folk are born *knowing* the language."

"The winds are kinder on warm days," Shya explained, wanting to make it clear that she wasn't entirely devoid of power. "I still can't understand what they whisper, not all of it, but I think they humor me, which means they must be able to understand me... at least a little. And on really hot days I can fly... though I'm not very good at it."

Kell looked thoughtful. "I wonder if something went wrong with your initiation."

Shya shook her head. "It was the same as everyone else's. My parents and Shaman Westwind thought of that. In case I was just a little slow, I had a second initiation." She didn't like to think about it. She couldn't remember the first one because she'd been too young. The second time haunted her. At night, she sometimes felt herself falling, and she knew everyone was watching, waiting for her to start flying. She always woke just as she reached the ground. "It didn't help." She'd broken both legs. That was when people started treating her differently.

The expression on Kell's face indicated that she was puzzling over the problem. "What does the wind feel like to you?"

"What does it *feel* like?" Shya shrugged. "It's wind. What's it supposed to feel like?"

Kell nodded. "I suppose that follows."

"Follows what?" Shya asked.

"If your magic isn't very strong, it's logical that the touch of wind doesn't do for you what it does for others." Kell gathered up the dishes and stood. "You see, to sky folk, fire is just hot. If you get too close to it, you'd pull back."

"Fire isn't hot to you?" She'd wondered how the fire folk could handle it.

Kell tipped her head to one side, then the other. "From a distance it feels hot. When I touch it, it's warm and soft. It's like the feeling you have when you wake up in the winter, but you're still all toasty warm under your blankets." She smiled. "The flames are my friends, and I can feel that when I touch them. I assume sky folk feel the breezes the same way."

Shya slouched in her chair. Not only had her stupid third spirit condemned her to a life essentially without magic, she would never know the touch of her element. She could have lived without that knowledge, and now that she had it, it would rankle and growing worse over time.

"We should be going," Kell said.

Shya stood up. "We?" she asked, looking at her hostess in confusion.

Kell nodded. "We had a bargain. I showed you my scrolls, and now you've got to show me yours." She gestured toward the door with one open hand. "Besides, I promised your parents I would bring you home after you'd eaten."

Once outside, Kell deposited the dishes in a water-filled basin in front of the neighboring wagon. A young woman poked her head out the window at the sounds, then smiled and waved. The fire shaman waved back, then dropped her hand to Shya's

12

shoulder.

"How do those wrists feel?" Kell asked as they walked through the encampment.

Shya held out her arms and gently rotated her hands. "A little stiff," she admitted, suspecting the woman would know if she lied. They ached with her pulse, but mentioning that would only be whining. Shya detested whiners.

None of the adult fire folk seemed to think it odd, the company their shaman kept. Bexa was with a group of fire children, and they passed a second mixed group of youths near the forest edge. Both times, the conversation had broken off as Shya and Kell approached, and she was certain it wasn't just her own clan who stared. At last, they reached her home tree.

The trees of the sky folk were enormous, their trunks wider than four wagons parked together. Although it was grooved, the bark was smooth, without cracks or flakes. The Skychild tree stood out from all the others, even those housing other sky folk. A case of wooden stairs circled the trunk up to the door. When being nasty, her siblings called it Shya's Path.

"*This* is to my liking," Kell said as she followed up the steps. "Fire folk don't fly. Not ever. And being helped up into one of your homes..."

Shya looked over her shoulder and saw the woman shake her head. "Is disquieting," she suggested.

"Much worse than that," Kell said with a laugh. "I'm used to being in control of myself and where I am." She shook her head again. "And I loathe heights."

Shya stopped, turning fully around. "You do?" she asked in surprise. This woman was stronger than anyone else Shya had met, yet something as simple as a distance from the ground unsettled her. It made her seem more real, but it also didn't quite seem possible. "But you have all that magic."

"Yes I do," Kell agreed. "But flying is very different from what I do, and all magics have limits."

Shya continued up the stairs, her thoughts everywhere and nowhere at the same time. What kind of reception would her guest get from her family? For once the stairs were useful and not merely a sign of shame. What savories were worthy of serving to a shaman of the fire folk? Who was home? Was she in trouble? Her room and shelves had better be neat.

Magic had limits.

* * *

Shya tried to shrug off the hands that shook her, thinking they were part of her dream. They persisted and were accompanied by a voice that made itself heard through her sleep-muddled mind.

"Wake up Shya," her mother said. "You have someplace to be this morning."

Shya groaned and opened her eyes. The room was dark, lit only by a candle, which meant the sun wasn't up yet. It was no wonder she was tired and difficult to wake. She'd sat up late with Kell, talking and looking over scrolls, as they'd done the last several nights. The fire folk would move on in a few days, which meant they had only so much time to share their favorites. Shaman Westwind had come looking for Kell when Shya had, at last, returned to the first tale Kell shared. He'd insisted on consulting with the fire shaman privately. Kell had clearly brushed aside his earlier requests, as well as those from others, and finally had to take the time to meet with him. Shya hoped there might still be time for her to finish that scroll.

"You're being a light breeze," her mother said in gentle chastisement. "Get up. You need to get dressed."

Shya sat up and pushed the covers away, noticing as she did, that her bandaged wrists didn't hurt. She wiggled them gently, as far as the wrappings would let her. They were still sore when pushed, but they were definitely better. She realized her mother was laying out her best clothing. "What's going on?" she asked, wondering if she'd missed something important in all her absences of late. "Where are we going?"

Her mother paused for a moment, then continued to rummage through Shya's socks. "I can't tell you where. You have a part in a ritual, and it's no small honor."

Shya would have guessed *that* from the fancy tunic her mother wore. Individual pearls and white glass beads made a swirling pattern reminiscent of wind across the front and back. Strands of pearls mingled with the long fringe on the underside of the sleeves. Shya's own dress clothes were more simple; white sheepskin pants with matching fringe running down the outside seams, and a matching shirt that hit the middle of her thighs. She had no beads or pearls. When she was older, she might have something fancier, but the fringe would never dance in the wind. Like her hair, the dangling bits of leather tangled instead of swirling prettily. The fringe was characteristic of her folk, not just her clan, but Shya's fringe was only about an inch long.

Something about her mother wasn't quite right, but Shya couldn't quite put her finger on what. It wasn't fear, exactly, but it wasn't sadness either. Worry was the closest thing Shya could come up with, though it wasn't the same kind of worry her mother exhibited when she caught Shya out on the big branch.

Papa waited at the bottom of the stairs. As he paced through the great room, looking every inch a proper sky folk, it was clear something troubled him as well.

"Where we going?" Shya asked. None of her siblings had been roused along with her, and she couldn't imagine what special event would involve *her* but not the others.

"To meet an unprecedented opportunity," he said. "Come along. We mustn't be late."

Shya expected her parents to fly wherever they were headed, with them pushing her along. Instead, her father went out the door and started down the stairs. She barely remembered him building them, and that had been the *only* time she'd ever seen him use them. She hurried to follow, her mother a few paces behind. "What's going on?" she asked once they were about halfway down the spiral. It was clear they were keeping something from her, but she couldn't guess what it might be.

For a long time, her only answer was silence. They were nearly to the ground when her father finally replied. "We have made an arrangement for you. More than that, I can't tell you at this time." Though Papa wasn't the type to speak without thinking, he seemed to be choosing his words more carefully than usual. "If things go well, you'll understand it all shortly."

His response raised more questions than it answered. An arrangement? She was the right age for her people to agree upon matches. The weddings, of course, took place years later. Shya's oldest sister had been promised at thirteen and would marry this summer, at seventeen. But she hadn't considered such things for herself. Who would seek to match their son with *her*? The answer was, too clearly, no one, and Shya wondered what other kinds of arrangements involved a ritual. She was too old for an apprenticeship and insufficiently skilled for anything else.

She walked between her parents, their boots rustling in last fall's soggy leaves. Although she went for walks as often as it was permitted, they moved into a part of the forest she was unfamiliar with.

"We love you," her mother said.

While Shya didn't doubt the sentiment, the words felt ominous instead of reassuring.

They walked for half an hour or longer, going farther from the village than she'd ever been alone, and she could feel the sun lurking just beyond the horizon. She heard low voices on the gentle breeze, but didn't recognize them. Then they entered a clearing, and she understood why. A small group of people were waiting, all fire folk in their formal dark red tunics and black pants, snug at the wrists and ankles. Despite her infirmity, Shya could sense the magic that saturated even the air she breathed.

In the low light, she recognized the fire clan chieftain and his wife. He raised a hand to Shya's parents in greeting as they approached. Two brawny big men she'd seen but never met stood nearby. Kell was also there, holding the tall black staff of a fire shaman. Her hair was back in two neat braids, while the other fire folk wore only one. Three horizontal stripes of yellow adorned her right cheek, and her left eye was circled in the same color. She glanced over Shya quickly, not meeting her eyes.

The ritual her parents mentioned must be one of the fire folk's. What purpose could she possibly serve? Why hadn't anyone prepared her? Perhaps her part was simple.

"The sun wakes," the chieftain said, nodding to Shya's parents. "If it is to be done, it is time." He bowed to Shya in a way that signified great respect, then slowly backed away.

She looked up at her parents in confusion as they each took one of her hands. "If *what* is to be done?"

"The ritual," Papa said as they led her farther into the clearing. "It's timed for sunrise."

In the very center was a fire pit large enough to roast a wild boar, ringed with stones. Fresh kindling and split firewood had been neatly stacked within. A taller log had been left, whole and standing upright, in the very center. It was the strangest thing she'd ever seen.

Her parents halted at the edge of the ring, staring into it without seeming to see. Now that she was closer, Shya could see that the firewood had been placed several inches away from the odd post in the center. She was no expert on building fires, but she supposed it could be characteristic of the fire folk. They didn't have to worry about their flames not catching, or about them spreading where they weren't wanted.

"It is needful for you to go into the center, Shya," Papa said, staring straight ahead. He dropped her hand, and a moment later her mother did the same. He slipped a small knife from its sheath at his belt and nonchalantly sliced through one of the thin strips dangling from his right pant leg. "Here," he said, giving Shya the fringe piece while handing the knife to his wife.

"What's this for?" Shya asked, pinching the long strip to hold it up.

"Take this as well," her mother said, holding out a beaded dangle still attached to a piece of leather fringe.

"Hang them on the post," her father said. "There should be some chains around the back you can tie them to."

"That's all I have to do?" Shya asked. So far it looked nothing like sky folk rituals, and she'd never heard of combining sky and fire magic. Could it even be done?

"Once you're there, we'll see what follows," he replied.

Off to one side, there was a gap in the kindling that made a suitable path. In the center, the ground was a little lower, and Shya could see that the end of the post had been buried to keep it standing straight. She walked around it, making an effort not to touch anything, lest she disturb something important. She found the two thick chains hanging on the back of the post. Like the clearing, the chains emanated magic, but they looked new, recently forged.

Shya slipped her father's fringe piece through one link in the middle of one chain. She tied it in a square knot, then did the same with her mother's fringe on the other chain. Perhaps they needed to be placed by one who wouldn't leave a hint of her own power on them. With her weak spirit, she was ideal for such a task. Finished, she walked the rest of the way around the post and looked over the firewood at her parents. They seemed farther away than they should have. For a moment she thought she saw tears on her mother's cheeks, but that couldn't be right. What reason would her mother have to cry? Her father's expression was blank, the way it was when he was trying to reign in a particularly intense feeling.

"Now what should I do?" she asked.

"Stand still for a moment," he instructed.

She stood and waited, trying to be both patient and very still. The chains on the other side of the post sprung to life with a rattle. When she would have stepped away, a strong gust of wind pressed her back against the upright log. One chain leapt over each of her shoulders, then crossed her chest to hold her fast. When they stopped moving, she looked up and saw that her mother's outstretched right hand controlled the wind.

"Mummie, what are you doing? What's happening?" Shya squirmed against the chains, but couldn't get loose. The same fear she felt in her dreams of falling gripped her. Her face grew hot, and her heartbeat pounded in her ears. Her parents stepped back, and the fire folk came closer. She couldn't hear Kell's words, and after a moment Shya was completely preoccupied by the flames that jumped from the hands of the fire folk onto the kindling.

Had she truly been so terrible that she had to be killed? Couldn't they just send her away, if her failure was too much to bear? She'd never read of such things, but the heat of the growing fire squashed any doubt of what was happening. She struggled to free herself, but the chains tightened, holding her more firmly against the post. By coincidence, the chains overlapped where she'd tied her parents' fringes. They twisted a little in the fire's breeze.

"Please! Don't do this, please!" Shya cried. "I don't know what I did to make you do this to me. But I'm sorry! Please, just let me go! I'll leave. I promise. I'll go away!"

One by one, the folk outside the circle turned their backs on her. The heat rising over the top of the orange flames distorted her parents' expressions as they turned away. Kell was the last to do so. For a moment, she very definitely met Shya's eyes. There was meaning in her expression, but Shya was unsure what it was. Then the shaman who had become her friend put her back to Shya.

The wood was dry, and the fire magically conjured, so the flames spread quickly. Shya sweated as she again tried to break free, although she was certain she couldn't escape even if she got loose. The fire was too big, too hot. There was no way out of her ring of flames. She whimpered as the heat surrounded her, closing her off from the rest of the world. Her life wasn't exactly charmed, but it was *hers*, and the only one she would get.

She begged her third spirit to help her, but it didn't listen. Instead of a breeze, hot tongues of flame lapped out, teasingly close but not yet touching her. Some of the piled firewood to her right collapsed with a crunch and a whoosh, sending sparks flying. The fire crawled among the falling bits to wrap around her ankle.

She took a deep breath, but her scream died unvoiced. The fire felt warm, not hot, as it slowly twined up her right leg. It spoke in a language of shifting light, heat, and soft sizzling noises. It would not harm her. It would burn things, heat things, and hurt others *for* her, but it would never hurt *her*. The flames were soft and comfortable, not sharp as she expected. Then she remembered Kell's words. *The flames are my friends, and I can feel that when I touch them.*

Shya took a slow deep breath, calling the fire that circled her. It came. It swarmed over her, sinking in and becoming part of her. She knew the nature of fire in a way that she had never understood the winds. She stood still for long moment, savoring the warmth and happiness she'd never known before. When she opened her eyes, she saw that she'd extinguished the fire, leaving cold coals and half charred wood behind. There wasn't even smoke. Then she noticed that she was naked, though her pale skin wasn't marked with ash or soot.

"I'm done," she called. "I think." She couldn't imagine that there would be anything else to the initiation than what she'd already gone through. If she weren't so happy, if her third spirit wasn't making itself so joyfully apparent, she would have been furious. Instead, she understood. No initiation was without its danger, and in time someone would explain why it needed to be done this way.

Kell was the first to look at her, and she was smiling. "I'll start teaching you to work metal this winter," she said. The chains relaxed and slipped away. She beckoned to Shya.

As the rest of the folk turned to watch her, Shya looked down at her feet, acutely aware of her nudity. She was much too old to parade around bare. She should have felt cold, she realized, but the fire she'd taken into herself warmed her.

Fabric was laid across her shoulders and she raised her head. The chieftain and his wife draped a red robe over her, helping her get her arms into the sleeves, and fastening the ties for her. He took Shya's face in both hands and kissed her on the cheeks. "We welcome you among us, my daughter," he said. "May your flame burn brightly for many years to come."

* * *

Shya tucked the last of her scrolls into the cabinet. She could hear her parents outside, talking to Kell. They'd seemed so torn in the last two days. She wasn't sick and weak anymore, but she was no longer sky folk. In truth, she had never been sky folk, and she didn't belong with them. They had to let her go, and they weren't happy about it.

"I don't think there's anything wrong with the way you named her," Kell said. "You called a third spirit, and one came. It just happened to be a fire spirit, instead of the expected sky spirit. It can happen." There was a pause. "That's why we had to do her initiation the way we did. Only that kind of fear, and desperation for survival, can awaken a spirit so long dormant." She'd given

20

Shya the same explanation, with more detail, on the walk back to the village after the ritual.

Shya felt it was well worth the fear, and she hadn't woken with fiery nightmares from the experience. The fire was inside her now, a part of her. She'd never be afraid of it. It was what her family felt about the wind, and it was something she could finally understand. *She* was no longer dormant.

Dragon Tale

Despite the heat of the day, the forest was cool. It was truly the only place to be, if one had any choice in the matter. Kevesh waded through the shallow stream, his great taloned feet sinking in the soft mud and sending out eddies of cloudy water behind him. Although he was one of the largest creatures in the forest, he watched where he walked. He carefully stepped over a painted turtle peering up at him with some concern.

"I see you, little shell-friend," he called softly, not wishing to disturb the forest with his usual booming voice.

Though most of the water in the slowly moving stream was stagnant, it was cool. Kevesh held his wings flat against his back as he pushed headlong between two pines at the water's edge. His scales protected him from the worst of the prickly branches, but it hurt to catch a wing that way. Yes, there it was. The hollow he'd dug into the side of the hill had grown thick with moss since his last visit. It would be a comfortable place to wait out the heat of the day. As he took a deep breath, nearby branches and fronds wafted toward him. He loved the smell of the forest in the summer. The only way he'd ever been able to describe it was 'green,' like wet ferns. But then, dragons weren't fond of fancy descriptions and gold-plated words.

As he settled himself on his bed of politrichum moss, he recognized the distinctive rounded leaves of wild mint. He grinned, then rubbed the side of his muzzle through the plants, smearing himself with the juice. It was turning out to be a perfect day.

He'd chosen this particular place because it was comfortable, yet it provided him with a variety of things to watch. At a hundred and fifty, he was too young to sleep a whole day through the way older dragons might. Water bugs skated across the surface of the stream and small pools of standing water. The thick full plants shook from the passage of a muskrat who occasionally stopped to snack on the varied flora. Every once in a while a bird would sing out, or squawk in protest, but this appeared to be a time of inactivity for them. A low bridge connected the well-worn dirt path that reached the stream on both sides. In the past he'd gotten to watch, unseen, as humans used the little bridge in their travels through the forest. He couldn't see the two frogs carrying on a conversation on the other side of the bridge; it was as well he wasn't a gossip. A red squirrel, chirping in alarm, ran partway up a nearby birch, turning to continue his harangue at an unseen opponent below.

Kevesh had just settled his head on his forearms when he heard the approaching hoof-beats of a horse. He grinned again. Humans were peculiar and fascinating creatures, and he'd spent a great deal of time trying to figure out just what they were all about. How he'd love to write a paper on their culture. He sighed. They spooked easily, making them difficult to research.

"Let me down!"

The sharp voice pulled Kevesh out of his contemplation. A delectable looking white steed paused at the edge of the bridge. Naturally, his master was a knight in shining plate armor. The protest had come from a young maiden squirming in the knight's arms.

"I said, let me go!" she shrieked, struggling against his

hold. Most of her sandy hair was pulled back in a braid, although some had come free to hang about her oval face.

The man laughed. "Do you think I care one way or the other what you say?" He tightened his arms around her. "You belong to me now, Mirabelle. The sooner you accept it the easier it will be."

"Belong to you?" she demanded. "I don't belong to anyone!" She pounded on his hands.

He laughed again.

Kevesh watched the man dismount, pulling the maiden with him. He'd never seen anything like this, but he'd always known that knights were despicable sorts and not to be trusted for an instant. There was a dull clank as the knight pulled off his helmet and dropped it nearby. His beard and mustache were blond, as was his cropped hair, and a ring of sweat circled his face. Holding Mirabelle by the back of her head, he kissed her. Although for a moment, Kevesh thought the man was trying to eat her face.

Mirabelle started to cry. "Leave me alone."

"You're mine, Mira. And you're far too fine to leave alone." He ran his dagger through the laces of her bodice, and with a swift jerk, the blade cut through.

"But, you're a *knight*," she protested tearfully.

He grinned at her, the kind of grin that raised the spines on Kevesh's back. "Of course I'm a knight." He kissed her again. "What did you expect?"

"You're supposed to help people," she insisted, pushing at his armor-clad chest.

"And I am." There was that grin again. "I'm helping myself."

She managed to get a hold of her emotions for a moment. "I've no wish to marry you, Sir Lavine," she said, managing to sound very formal and self-assured.

He laughed, and Kevesh had to stifle the low growl he wanted to let out. "I'm not going to marry you Mira. But if I like you enough, I may keep you a while."

"My father will kill you!" She batted at his hands as he worked the fastenings of her light blue skirt.

24

"He'll do no such thing," Sir Lavine corrected her quietly. "I resolved his little sheep theft problem and he owes me. He knows it." He chuckled at his success, and her skirt slipped to the ground. He placed a heavy foot on it, preventing her from pulling it back on.

Her face was twisted in anger. "The thieves were a couple of starving children."

The knight shrugged. "That doesn't matter. I caught them, and when he finds you gone, he'll know I've taken my reward." He took advantage of her shock to loosen the tie of her full-length chemise, which slipped to her waist as the sleeves caught on her hands.

She belatedly tried to cover herself as Sir Lavine fought her quick hands. In the struggle, Mirabelle lost her chemise, but Sir Lavine lost his hold on her, and she scrambled toward Kevesh's forest resting place.

"You can't run away from me Mira. Where will you hide in the big dark forest?" He followed, not quite at a run.

Mirabelle nearly ran into Kevesh before she saw him, and he abruptly sat up. She stood frozen with fear.

"I won't hurt you," Kevesh whispered.

"But you're a *dragon*," she protested in a whisper, her earlier plight momentarily forgotten.

"I suppose you think dragons eat people," he said. "That's about as accurate as knights in shining armor rescuing the weak and downtrodden out of the goodness of their hearts." He got to all four feet and pulled her toward him. It was to her credit that she didn't scream or faint. "Stand behind me, and I'll see what I can do about this knight of yours."

Sir Lavine pushed through the trees and stared at Kevesh for a moment, completely stunned. "Run Mira!" he shouted. Trained reflexes springing to action, he jerked his sword from it's scabbard. "It'll eat you!"

Kevesh let out a deafening roar, and the entire forest seemed to go silent. Sometimes it was nice to be a dragon. "The lady Mirabelle will not be taking any more of your advice, Sir whatever you call yourself." He casually batted the sword out of the knight's hand. As the knight ran toward his horse, equally panicked by the sight of a dragon, Kevesh followed, stomping his feet in an excess of draconic glee. Yes indeed, these were the times when it was terrific to be a dragon.

Once he was sure the man was gone, and not likely to come back with one of those stupid poking sticks, which could be quite a problem if one wasn't careful, Kevesh carefully picked up the discarded clothes. He brushed them off as gently as his claws would permit, and turned back toward his hollow. Mirabelle was peeking out from behind the trees, watching him. Her eyes were a lovely green, and he was surprised to see the color in a human face. Perhaps they weren't so different after all.

"I imagine you'll want these back," he said, holding out her clothes. Humans were exceedingly odd about concealing their bodies. Kevesh had often wondered if it was a necessary adaption to protect what appeared to be very thin skin, or if it was the result of one of their bizarre religions.

She stepped forward, still timid, and took her clothes. She quickly pulled on her white chemise, all the while thanking him profusely for his assistance. "I don't know what I would have done if not for you..." she paused suddenly. "You do have a name, don't you?"

"I'm Kevesh," he said with a nod.

"Well, Kevesh, I don't know that a dragon has any use for the aid of a human, but is there anything I can do for you?"

"You mean that?" he asked. On his few close encounters with humans, most couldn't wait to get as far from him as possible.

She nodded, smiling.

Kevesh thought about his paper. "Would you come home with me? I've a research project I could really use your help with."

"Go home with you?" she asked hesitantly. "You mean, to live with you?"

"Oh yes. For a little while at least."

"I don't know. It isn't quite what I had in mind."

"We could have lots of fun, and I'd get to do my research. The elders have been telling me for years that there's no way I'll finish my project. If you'll help me..." Just considering the implications made him shake his head. "I have some very good ideas, and I suspect it could be beneficial to people too." He refrained from using his normal persuasive expression. She might just run off to find that stupid knight, thinking him less frightening.

She thought about it "I can't really go home. After the way I disappeared, what would they think?"

"Please come with me, lady Mirabelle?"

Swallowing the last of her hesitation, she gave him a low curtsey. "It would be an honor to assist you in your research."

"Well then, why don't you hop on?" He looked pointedly to his back.

She stared at him a moment. "You mean, ride you?"

"It would take a long time to get to my home if you were to try it on foot. The mountain would surely be impossible." He crouched down. "Flying's fun, Mirabelle. You'll like it." He let his enthusiasm creep into his voice. Flying was another great thing about being a dragon.

He directed her to use his front leg as a step up to his back, just to the front of his wings. Although she seemed a bit unsure of the concept, she was very cooperative. He was a little more than twice the size of a good war horse and he suspected she was used to riding horses.

"What do you eat?" Kevesh asked, wondering if they would need to stop somewhere on the way. "I've never had an occasion to dine with a person before."

"Oh, I'll eat most any vegetables, fish or meat..." She paused. "What do you eat?" her voice was uncertain.

His graceful neck allowed him to look at her even as she sat astride him. "Certainly not people." He made a face. "Too many small bones to get stuck in your throat. And it's a long throat to have things stuck in. Besides, I hear humans cause bloating, and it's a bad idea for a fire breather to get gas."

"Oh," she looked surprised.

"I eat a lot of meat though. I'm a pretty good hunter," he said with a bit of pride. He began walking them out of the forest then.

"So you *don't* eat people, but you *do* breath fire," she said, as if trying to reconcile fact with myth.

"Correct."

"Can you really see halfway across the planet?"

He hadn't heard that one before. "Oh no. Dragons are actually quite nearsighted."

"But... I thought flying predators had to have good eyes for hunting."

He paused and flashed her a look. "You think I could make a meal out of a mouse?" He twitched his tail, a good length away, to indicate his size. "I just need to be able to spot a cow, or a sheep, and they're plenty big enough for me to see." He smiled.. "I think we have a lot to learn about each other. I hope you're up for the task."

"Oh, I am," she insisted quickly.

He brought them out of the forest then. "Hang on Mirabelle. Time for your first flying lesson." He could hardly wait to show her his home, and he was glad he'd tidied up earlier. He wasn't sure what humans were used to, and he hoped they could make some sensible compromises. The chance to have a human room-mate was just too fabulous to pass up. His neighbors would be so jealous.

"Are all knights like Sir Lavine?" she asked as they took to the air.

It was the perfect time to dispel myths. "Trust me. I've seen my share of knights, and they're no good."

Dream Walker

Many years ago, before your grandparents' grandparents were born and many years again before that, the world was more wild than tame, and people known as the Jha made their home in the land of wide plains, large forests, and tall mountains. Food was plentiful and the tribes routinely traded with each other so they need not migrate with the seasons. In a Jha village in the center of the Great Forest lived a girl named Shruti. Able to see things no one else could, it was said that she would become a powerful shamanka. The expectation that she might surpass all other shamanka, even those in legend, was nearly more than she could stand. At thirteen, her abilities were not entirely hers to command. Birendra, the village shaman and her teacher, had simply smiled when she confessed her lack of self-confidence.

"You are more wise than you realize," he said, handing her an amethyst crystal as long and thin as her own pinky finger. It was tightly wrapped with sinew at the broken end, and there was a loop large enough to slip over her head. "Only a fool would think herself perfect at your age. You're young, and your control will improve in time. If you don't get lost, you will surely become more powerful than me."

Unsettled by his words, Shruti frowned and fingered the purple crystal. "What's this?"

"Just wear it for now," he said, giving her the closed look that meant she would get no answers today. "In time you will learn to use it, but only once you have become attuned to it."

She wrinkled her nose in annoyance, but knew better than to push when Birendra gave answers like that. He was the most stubborn person she'd ever met. "Everyone thinks I'm as good as you already," she said, returning to her original complaint. It wasn't fair. Her sister Priyanka was fifteen and training to be a huntress. No one would have imagined asking her to join the ranks of the seasoned Jha so soon. While Shruti knew nothing about the way of the huntress, she could tell Priyanka was getting better all the time. She wished she could say the same for herself. "I try so hard, but it doesn't make a difference."

"It may seem that way," Birendra said as he settled himself on a woven grass mat on the dirt floor of his hut. He crossed his long skinny legs. Like most men, he lived alone, and Shruti happened to know that it had been a long time since he had been invited to share a woman's hut. A young man and a boy near her age both possessed Birendra's long nose and deep set eyes, though neither of them had a shaman's gifts. "Trust that I have seen progress," he said.

Shruti dropped down to her own mat, on the opposite side of a small stone fire ring from him. She held in her grumbles, but her discontent must have shown on her face.

"Could you dream walk a year ago?" he asked, clearly proving a point.

She shook her head. A year ago, she'd been terrified of the very idea, and it had taken all of Birendra's coaxing to convince her to try. Now, she did it all the time, seeking answers to village problems and heeding warnings to take back to the elders. Sometimes she watched the weather for storms or searched the forest for the greatest animal populations. A shamanka could protect her people from predators and help find food while preventing the over-hunting that led some to starvation.

"What you're doing takes more time than other skills," he said. "It's slow. But you're learning. We can ask no more." He sprinkled grated farsight root onto the large flat stone in the center of the fire. Pungent smoke rose to fill the hut.

Shruti picked up her wooden bowl, half full of clear water she'd fetched earlier from the nearby stream. She dipped her fingers into the cool liquid, then sprinkled droplets onto the stone, coals and all. It sizzled and steamed.

"Now, let us walk together," Birendra suggested.

* * *

Shruti's feet were strangely noiseless as she moved through the darkened forest. She'd lost Birendra, but something kept her from calling out for him. It was an overcast night; no moonlight shone through the gaps in the trees. Though she was no huntress, she knew something was wrong. The forest was never silent, not the way it was now.

When first learning to dream walk, she hadn't wanted to fully surrender to the dreams. She'd been terrified of becoming lost in the place that was both inside her mind and out in the wide world. While some folk who lost their path found the way back, most didn't. Holding back didn't work well, either, since it doused one or more of her senses. Sometimes she couldn't smell, other times she'd been unable to see. It hadn't happened in months, and she nearly stamped her foot in the stilled forest, angry with herself for failing at something so basic. She was sure she'd let go completely. But if so, why had she left her hearing behind... or had she? She held her palms together and rubbed them, near her face. The sound was soft, but it was there. That was only slightly reassuring. The silence was not right.

She paused and closed her eyes, listening with all her might. Nothing. A chill washed over her and she looked down at her feet for assurance. A small brown rabbit sat behind her heels, shadowing her. The rabbit was her anchor; the guide who could always find the way to the living world. Everyone who walked in dreams had such a creature, though it was bad luck to speak its name with others. If she were parted from the rabbit, or if she

31

ignored its advice, Shruti could easily lose her way. The path to waking was much like the others and it was easy to take the wrong one.

She'd walked alone often enough that she should have felt comfortable, but she was as nervous as if it were her first time. Taking a deep breath, Shruti continued moving, letting her feet take her where they would. She always ended up where she needed to be, and found her way faster if she didn't try to make the decisions consciously.

A breeze she could barely feel wafted a foul smell in her direction. The odor of a dead beast gone to carrion mixed with the scent of the festering mud pools of the big swamp. It grew stronger with each step, and she gagged. She paused, breathing through her mouth to see if she could bear to continue on.

Click, click, click.

The sound echoed through the unnatural quiet.

Click, click, click.

It was louder, closer. The horrible stink got worse, and she could almost taste it. She pulled the neck of her hide shirt up to cover her nose.

"Nwebetay. Nwebetay," something whispered up ahead, from the same direction as the clicking. It was low and angry. "Nwebetay, nwebetay."

It was no animal sound, yet it wasn't language. What did it mean? Was she too far away to hear properly? Was it the utterance of something dying? Was it a warning? She took cautious steps forward.

"Nwebetay. Nwebetay." Click, click, click. Leaves rustled and small sticks cracked under weight.

Shruti froze. It was coming toward her. She wanted to duck behind one of the great trees, but if this was what she had come for, it would find her no matter where she went.

"Nwebetay. Nwebetay."

She gagged at the stench, barely able to stand. The branches in front of her shook, hard.

"Nwebetay, nwebetay, nwebetay," it said quickly. It leaped out from between two trees, breaking off limbs the size of Shruti's

32

arm in passing. It was twice as tall as a full-grown woman, and in the dark, its skin seemed black and shiny, hard like the shell of a poison turtle. It had two sets of arms, the lower ones ending in four clawed fingers, and the upper ones with pincers like a mud crab. Its mouth was larger than those of the big cats, and it hung open, drooling. Tusks jutted out unevenly from between two upper teeth, on the sides. Its great fat tongue, like a giant writhing slug, slid over the points of its teeth as it looked down at Shruti.

"Nwebetay, nwebetay!" Its pincers clicked together.

Shruti screamed, then stumbled as she took a step backward. Her butt and hands hit the ground. The little brown rabbit crouched under the bend of her legs. Her link to home. She grabbed it with both hands, clumsily mashing the soft fur with her fingers, just as the monster reached for her ankle with one of its clawed paws.

She shuddered and, feeling herself held tight, thrashed in panic. "No!" She pushed and kicked, trying to squirm away from her captor. Her cheek stung from a slap.

"Open your eyes, Shruti," a man said, his voice urgent. "Open your eyes!" He slapped her again.

She did as she was told, blinking and gulping in confusion. She was with Birendra, in his hut, not in the forest. They'd been dream walking. She clung to the front of his shirt, burying her face in the soft hide. She was out of breath, as if she'd been running. "What was it?" she finally asked, looking up at him when she felt herself firmly back in the living world.

He shook his head. "You'll have to tell me. You lost me again."

She closed her eyes and sighed. She had failed the exercise.

"I don't think it's your fault," he said, moving back to his mat across from her. "You have begun to go places I can't. We'll just have to figure out to where that boundary is, so you cross it only when you mean to, and so we can walk together when we wish."

Shruti nodded, both relieved and unsettled.

"Now tell me what you saw. Your dreams are true, and if it

was bad, I must know so I can warn the elders if there is need."

* * *

"One of the hunters is missing," Priyanka said as she handed Shruti a bowl.

"Missing?" their mother asked, placing a clay pot on a thick mat on the floor near the girls. It was supper time, when Jha families came together for the day.

Priyanka nodded. "He went out yesterday afternoon, and hasn't been seen since."

"Maybe he's sick," her mother suggested. "Not seeing him for a day doesn't mean he's missing."

"We checked his hut," Priyanka said dismissively. "His spear and knife were gone."

"Do you think he got lost?" her mother asked, her eyes darting to Shruti before returning to her oldest daughter.

Priyanka looked doubtful. "He was a hunter, Ma."

"Have the elders been told?" their mother asked, almost sounding unconcerned.

"Yes. We've been extra careful since Shaman Birendra warned us." Priyanka also glanced at her sister. "We're going looking for him tomorrow, but I don't think we'll find anything." She uncrossed her long tan legs only to re-cross them.

"Why not?" her mother asked. "If one of the big cats got him, there'd be something left."

"I don't think it was a big cat." Priyanka scooped the hot rice and fish into her bowl, careful to avoid getting too many sliced orange roots. "I think it was the Nwebetay."

Shruti stared at her sister, so matter of fact in her recounting. "Why? Did someone see it?" She'd desperately hoped her dreams had been wrong this one time, if never again.

Priyanka shook her head. "No. It's just a feeling I have." She tapped the center of her chest. "I hope it has finally come. I hate waiting. I'd rather fight it and get it over with."

* * *

The first person to see the Nwebetay and live to tell of it was a woman whose little boy was taken from the bank of the stream. She was fishing upwind from her child, and didn't see or

34

smell the Nwebetay until the boy screamed. The monster was exactly as Shruti had described. It hunted both day and night, though it stayed out of the village itself and preyed mostly on those who were alone. The hunters who disappeared were never found.

A huntress group tracked the Nwebetay for ten days, and two never returned. The survivors came back with bruises, deep cuts, and broken bones. Shruti had been correct about the monster's shell-like skin, and their weapons had been useless. Spears fractured and staffs did nothing. With the creature prowling near the village, it was too dangerous to hunt individually, but the smaller game animals the forest Jha typically ate were more difficult to catch in a group. Snares were often found sprung, but empty or with their catch dismembered.

At first mothers told terrible stories about the Nwebetay, to keep their children near, but some were intrigued by the tales instead of frightened. Filled with ignorant courage, they went off in search of the monster. A few of them made it back to the village, shaken and badly hurt. Aiswarya, one of Shruti's age mates and friends, lost three of the fingers on her strong hand. Buta, a boy who had timidly kissed Shruti at the spring festival, didn't survive the night. After that, the stories weren't needed. Both children and adults stayed close.

Shruti and Birendra took daily dream walks, hoping to discover a way to slay the Nwebetay. Since it wasn't the time of year when they had food stored, there was soon noticeably less to eat. The elders discussed sending hunters to the Open Plains, a journey that would take seven full days with little time to rest. The larger animals would feed more people, but the heavy meat would be difficult to get back to the village. They talked about seeking aid from other Jha tribes, but decided it was too dangerous to send the hunters away.

Finally, after many weeks and more deaths than the village could bear, the hunters chose to seek the Nwebetay, and overwhelm it with their full number. Eventually, its hard shell would break under their clubs and staffs. One of their spears would find a soft spot to pierce. All things had a weakness, and perhaps they could find it, if there were enough of them. They took even those in training, some of whom had just begun. Priyanka looked so proud on the morning she left. As Shruti watched the hunters go, she wondered if she would ever see her sister again.

* * *

"You've already helped," Birendra said firmly. "You warned the village."

"That's not enough," Shruti insisted. They'd been dream walking again. Although she was supposed to be walking with him, she'd knowingly gone where he couldn't follow. Since that had been where she'd seen the Nwebetay, she thought she would find the solution there. Her teacher wanted her to work on control and was annoyed when she intentionally disobeyed him.

"You can't do everything," he said. "And you shouldn't try to."

"There has to be something I can do," she said, frustrated.

"There is," Birendra agreed. "You can do your lessons as instructed, and learn how to use your talents. You won't be able to help anyone if you get lost in your own mind."

"What good are my talents?" she demanded, losing her temper at last.

The shaman was silent for a moment. "They're a lot better than you realize." He held up his hand when she took a breath to interrupt. "The Nwebetay is your creature, Shruti."

She froze and stared at him in confusion. "Mine?"

Birendra nodded. "It is your fear given form." He touched his forehead once, then held out his hand to indicate the world. "You have been very uncertain, and as proof of your strength you now have the ability to bring things into being. The first time is almost always an accident."

"I made the Nwebetay?" Shruti's voice was a whisper, and she had to work to force out the words. "You mean this is all my fault? And you knew this would happen?"

His hands folded around hers. "It's not your fault because you did not mean for it to be."

"People have been hurt... killed!" she wailed. "People I know."

"I'm sorry you must bear this pain," he said, his voice calm and even. "While the situation varies, this is something shaman and shamanka must all face in their turn."

The words made sense, though she wished they didn't. "Even you?" she asked quietly. It had never occurred to her that he might have suffered in his lifetime. He'd always seemed so content.

Birendra nodded. He said nothing for a moment. "You must defeat the Nwebetay, just as I faced the creature formed of my fears. The hunters may find a way to slay it, but then you will lose some of your power. If you defeat it, you will retain your full power. You can find its weakness by choice rather than chance. The elders know this."

She gasped in horror. She'd be thrown out. How could they permit her to stay?

Birendra squeezed her hands. "It is worth this danger to have a strong shamanka. You will learn and grow from this, and you will never again pose a risk to the village. You can do so much more than I to help our people. You can find answers that remain hidden from me." He paused to let his reassurance sink in, then followed with a caution. "Your powers are taking on their adult strength, Shruti. If you can not control them, they will destroy you. Being lost is nothing compared to this."

She let out a heavy breath, very near to tears. "Why didn't you warn me?"

"Would you have wanted to know?" He shook his head. "You would have inhibited yourself, and the risk to us all would be even greater. Even once I knew you had brought the Nwebetay, you were not yet prepared to deal with it. You did not have the necessary skills."

She looked away, not ready to admit he was right. "What do I have to do?" she asked, trying to set aside his words for later. It was too much all at once.

"You must learn control, quickly," he said. "And above all, be careful. The Nwebetay will follow if you leave. If it kills you, it will vanish, but then those who have died will have done so for no purpose because your power will be lost to us forever."

"How... how did you do it?" she asked timidly. "When you had to do this?"

He shook his head. "My solution will not help you, as each of us are different. The lesson you will take from this will be most valuable to you alone."

That evening Shruti felt herself slipping into a dream without any preparation. Frightened, she pulled out before the dream could truly take hold. One day she would be able to dream walk as Birendra could, without the aid of farsight root. As a fully trained shamanka, she might even learn to dream walk while doing other things. It increased the risk that she would be unable to wake from the dream, so she wasn't eager to try it.

"Are you all right?" her mother asked.

Shruti nodded. "I'm tired."

Her mother nodded. "You've been working so hard."

"I have to," Shruti said. It was as if she and her mother had made some silent agreement not to discuss the danger Priyanka faced. It wasn't even dark when she lay down on her pallet to go to sleep.

* * *

She stood in the forest, and after a few steps Shruti realized that she had crossed from sleep into a walking dream. She hadn't known such a thing could happen. Was it part of growing into her powers or was she destroying herself? She was solidly in the dream, so the only way out was through her guide. She looked around, but for once the rabbit wasn't near her feet. Her chest went tight with panic, and for a moment she couldn't breathe. She frantically cast about, searching for her guide. She'd always been able to find the rabbit without effort, whenever she wanted. Birendra's guide wasn't as helpful, she recalled. She'd seen the tiny wren dart out of his reach from time to time when they'd walked together, and he said the bird had only gotten more tricksy with time. Guides liked to have their games, he'd explained. Perhaps that was all there was to it. She dropped to her hands and knees to look under low branches as she tried to remember what Birendra had told her about finding a tricksy guide.

Click, click, click.

She froze. She hadn't been here before, but she recognized the eerie silence.

"Nwebetay. Nwebetay." It was a faint whisper as if from far off.

She held her breath, frightened. She'd tried to find the monster for weeks. Now that she knew where it had come from, she was even more desperate to learn what she could from the dream world. She couldn't leave now, even if her guide returned.

"Nwebetay, nwebetay, nwebetay." Click, click. It was closer, moving fast.

Her sister had gone out to slay the Nwebetay, the least Shruti could do was face it here. She had created it, and she had to get rid of it. She didn't feel ready. She wasn't strong enough. There was still so much to learn. She tried telling herself that such thoughts had brought the Nwebetay, and if she wasn't careful she might make it worse.

She lurched to her feet. "Nwebetay!" she called, cupping her hands around her mouth to make the sound carry. "Nwebetay!"

"Nwebetay, nwebetay!" it growled, charging out of the dark. It smelled worse, which didn't seem possible. It was slobbering and snorting. "Nwebetay, nwebetay!" it snarled.

With the monster raging in front of her, Shruti could no longer remember why she'd tried so hard to find it. She was young and small, no match for the vicious Nwebetay who had defeated her tribe's hunters. It didn't have a weakness. The hard shell skin covered its entire body. Its eyes were tiny, and even a good marksman would find them difficult targets. If a huntress could get within reach of its eyes, she would be within reach of its mouth, and those four arms. How had she created so hideous a thing? If her fears given form looked like this, what did it say of her?

"Nwebetay." It stepped slowly toward her.

Soft laughter filled the air, and the monster stopped, its great ugly head moving about. The sound swelled, echoing throughout the trees. The Nwebetay shrieked, its four arms flailing, then turned and ran back the way it had come. Shruti could see no one else in the forest, and she was sure trees could not laugh. But she'd learned that the truths of the waking world did not always apply to dream walking. As she looked about, hoping to discover more, she found her guide at her heels. Relieved beyond words, Shruti bent to pick her up, and the little brown rabbit chuckled, a very human sound.

Shruti opened her eyes and was blinded by the early morning sun was shining through the window onto her face. She jumped to her feet and dressed as quickly as she could. She needed to talk to Birendra, now. He would know how to find the hunters, and she had to reach them before the Nwebetay. She ran the short distance to the hut where she spent most of her waking hours. "Birendra," she called, knocking once on the frame before pushing aside the hide that covered the entrance.

Startled awake, the shaman sat up, his covers in disarray and his eyes wide. "What? What's wrong?"

He looked alarmed when she told him about the unplanned walk she'd taken, but he sat in silence until she finished. "I know you can't find the Nwebetay," she said, "but can you find the hunters? Where there's one, I think I'll find the other."

Birendra nodded, his face grave. "I can, and I will. But you must promise me two things first."

Shruti nodded.

He held up one finger. "Be careful, and I don't just mean in the living world. Today's need forces you to take up a new and dangerous skill without time to perfect it." He held up the second finger. "When you get home, you will work on your control. Your power has sprung into its mature form. This is a time when you will master it, or it will master you."

* * *

Shruti ran through the forest, twigs snatching at her arms and legs as she went. Her feet hurt and every breath made her throat burn. Finally, she paused, lifting her leather water bottle to her lips. After a few sips, she slipped lightly into a dream, wrapping her hand around the finger-sized amethyst crystal around her neck. It had once been longer and pointed at both ends, but Birendra had broken it in two. The halves sought each other, still thinking themselves whole. She could follow their voices through the dream over distance, to her teacher. They would not be together as they were on their walks, but she could hear his voice.

Birendra told her to stay on the overgrown trace and turn after she passed a small pond with several gray birds swimming across it. She released the crystal and took another mouthful of water before continuing on.

Before Birendra told her she was halfway there, she was already more tired than she'd ever been. She had to stop often to rest and make sure she was going the right way. Each time she worried about the delay. She couldn't help but think of Priyanka facing the Nwebetay. Shruti tried to keep taking sips of water, as Birendra had instructed, but after a while she felt like she was going to throw up. Still, she kept running. She knew she was getting close when she reached for Birendra the last time. She caught the sick stench of the Nwebetay, though it was faint. He urged her to hurry. He feared the Nwebetay had reached the hunters first.

She wished his words could give her new energy, but she was exhausted and there was nothing left. Weeks of light meals left her without any reserve and she was a shamanka not a huntress. It was all she could do to trudge up the last hill. She looked down into a shallow dip where the hunters fought the Nwebetay. Several lay on the ground, dead or unconscious, while those who still stood surrounded the monster and beat at it with their spears. Priyanka made several bold thrusts for its face with the knife end of her long staff. Ignoring the other hunters, the Nwebetay turned toward the young huntress, claws and pincers outstretched.

"Laugh," Shruti whispered. She didn't dare distract her sister with a shout, but what she needed to do was easier said than done. She searched her mind for anything that had ever amused her, something she'd seen, even a joke. She couldn't think anymore, she was so tired. She sank to her hands and knees. "Laugh."

The brown rabbit sat between her hands. "Don't think about them," she said in a voice no rabbit ever had. "I'll make you laugh."

Dazed, Shruti leaned back, focusing on the rabbit. "Have you always been able to talk?"

The rabbit shrugged, her round eyes holding Shruti's. "Do you want to talk, or do you want to laugh? We haven't time for both."

"I need to laugh," Shruti replied.

The rabbit reached behind herself with one paw, gave a tug and held up her detached cottontail. She leaned forward and pounded on the back of her head until both her eyeballs popped out. She scooped them up off the ground and started juggling her body parts. She hopped from foot to foot singing a tale about a creature that was half turkey and half toad.

Although Shruti had seen some very strange things while dream walking, this was by far the most absurd. A giggle escaped her lips. It was followed by another, harder. The more she thought about it, the sillier her guide was. She trusted this creature to take her home, to keep her from getting lost inside her own mind. A rabbit who juggled her eyes and ripped off her tail without a moment's thought. A rabbit with odd notions of what made good music. She trusted her sanity and her life to a trickster. Just slightly more hysterical than amused, Shruti laughed out loud, barely hearing the screams of the Nwebetay. She laughed until her stomach hurt and she could barely breathe. She no longer needed to look at her guide to keep laughing.

When she looked up at last, Shruti found herself still half in a dream, one she hadn't truly called. She reached for her guide with both hands, pausing before touching the soft fur. She'd always thought of the rabbit as an invention of her mind, not a real creature. But her mind could call things into being, and just because the rabbit was present in the dream didn't make her less real. It also didn't make her Shruti's invention. Her face burned with embarrassment when she recalled the rough handling her guide had endured.

"May I?" she asked. In response, the rabbit hopped into her hands.

When Shruti opened her eyes again, Priyanka was helping a wounded hunter to his feet and the Nwebetay was nowhere to be seen. The others knew she was there, though in a show of respect and awe they would not meet her eyes. She swallowed the sudden sense of shame. She'd brought death and fear to her people; they honored her for it. It felt wrong, no matter what Birendra had said. She was not sure her power was worth this great price, paid by others. She did not deserve to be honored by her people, and she wondered if she could ever feel worthy.

* * *

The Nwebetay never returned to bother the Jha again, for once such a creature has been defeated by its maker, it loses the power to harm. The Nwebetay fled to a deep cave, where it still lives to this day. The only things to eat in that dark place are the fish with no eyes who live in an underground pool. It flees from the sounds of happy people, but sometimes travelers through the High Mountains can hear the echo of, "nwebetay. Nwebetay."

Common Magic

Rivel woke to the rhythmic sound of waves lapping at the shoreline. He considered opening his eyes, but a hazy memory of pain associated with vision made that seem an unwise choice. He would find out what he could from his other senses before trying that avenue again.

His cheek rested against a coarse board. From the splinters and rough edges, he assumed it was old wood. It took a moment for him to realize he was rocking with the waves, and that nearly caused him to look after all. His right hand dangled into the water, which felt neither cold nor warm. He must be on a raft of some sort, and he was sprawled across the widely-spaced weather-beaten planks. His lips were dry, but there was no taste of brine, so he suspected he was on a lake. How he'd gotten there was less important than *where* he actually was.

He could hear a variety of bird calls, so he had to be relatively near land. The only identifiable scents were those of clean water and wet sand. He was far from the city, then. When he tried to reach out with his mind, he could sense nothing, and that *did* make him open his eyes.

He sat up. His head ached, a bit more than the rest of his body, and he felt as if he'd been beaten all over with a stick. He rubbed his eyes, but that didn't fix the blurriness, and he pushed down his panic by trying to figure out what had happened. It was mid-evening, to judge from the pale purple hue to the sky. The sun was in its gradual decline so he had a few hours yet before full dark. His raft was a small wooden platform atop four large casks, and he was floating about thirty lengths from a steep incline of shore. There was a crooked wooden stairway leading down the bank to a short dock off to his left. The water was clear, with a sandy bottom, which meant it could be a pleasant shallow wade, or lengths over his head. He wasn't up for a swim.

His fingers went to his neck, and he closed his eyes in anguish. His crystal was gone.

His memory of the previous night was a jumble. He'd gotten into a bar fight, probably over something stupid since that was his routine. And now here he was, Rivel Chamwell M4 apprentice, robbed of his most valued possession and dumped on a raft in a lake. The academy was in the port city Trevia on the Alzan sea, and other than the trip to the academy four years ago, he'd never traveled. He didn't even know where the nearest lake was.

As his brain feebly tried to function, he realized that if he didn't get back in the next day or so, he was going to miss his final exam, the test that led to graduation and the full title of magus. If he missed the exam, he'd have to take the whole year over, if the masters saw fit to give him a second chance. If not, he'd remain an M4, not the most employable sort of mage, forever. His parents spent years' of savings to send him to the academy. He was to be the family's first magus. The first from the village, in fact. They'd been so proud when he'd tested as talented. They'd be utterly humiliated if he returned in failure.

The masters had warned him his conduct was unsuitable. He drank too much and fought too much. He was far too friendly with the local tavern women. His extracurricular pursuits left little time for studying. How were they to make a proper magus out of him if he didn't cooperate? They'd kept him because his talent made up for his other inadequacies. While he'd no control over his abduction, he had to admit he wasn't free of blame. He couldn't think of a way to convince the masters he deserved another chance, and trying just made his headache worse.

He sighed. While the chance they'd welcome him back wasn't something he would have put money on, finding his way back to Trevia and the academy was his only good option. He couldn't give up on a magus rating without trying. He'd put too much into it, and while studying didn't thrill him, using his magic did.

He'd been drifting toward shore, and it would only be few more minutes before he could get off the raft. The early summer breeze was gentle, almost hesitant, and he fidgeted while wondering if anyone missed him yet. He guessed he'd been gone a whole night and most of a day, and that wasn't like him. If the masters liked him, they'd be worried, and that might help his cause. He couldn't rely on that, though. He'd most likely alienated the lot of them. He was grateful that the extra time he'd spent unconscious had killed off his hangover. He had a lump the size of a crab-apple on the back of his head, which probably accounted for what he remembered about the first time he'd come to. He wasn't hungry, and the idea of eating made him queasy. He leaned over the side of the raft to collect water in one hand. It was a tedious way to drink, but he was incredibly thirsty.

He felt the casks rub against the sandy bottom, beaching the raft a few lengths from the steep bank. He took off his black cloak. It was none too clean, which may have explained why it hadn't been taken when he'd been stripped of his crystal and belt pouch. He had none of his magical tools, and he cringed at the thought of the morons who'd sacked him trying to use them. He spread out his cloak, placing his tall black boots in the center, and made a tight bundle of it. Then he rolled his breeches to his knees and cautiously slipped off the edge of the raft.

The water reached the middle of his shins, and it was a little chilly. He slowly made his way to the dock. The stairs were far more inviting than the steep embankment. Placing his bundle on the dock, he cupped his hands to splash his face. He had scratches on the cheek that rested on the raft, and his jaw felt sore. He didn't remember getting popped in the face, but he must have, either before or after getting knocked on the head. He couldn't recall much of the evening or the fight. His reflection was translucent, more of a shadow, and his curly black hair was like a halo about his head. He wetted his hands and ran them over his hair, trying to flatten the curls.

At the top of the stairs he found a trail into the forest. It eventually intersected a wider gravel path. He stared down the path in each direction, uncertain which way to go. There were no signs, and he wondered exactly where he was. He didn't think he could be too far from the city, but was he close enough to get back in time for his final? Not if he went the wrong way.

Under normal circumstances he would use a directional spell, but without his crystal he couldn't focus his energy sufficiently to perform the spell. Why did mages have to be bound to a stupid rock? Oh but he missed his, though.

He wondered if it really had to be a clear, single terminated crystal point. True, crystals were the most powerful of all earth elements; they were the most pure. But all apprentices heard stories about the power of common stones within their first year at the academy. While the academy forbade experimentation with stone magic, the masters couldn't dismiss its existence. He suspected he'd lack the focus of his crystal, but perhaps he could find something that would do, at least to get him home.

He crouched down and ran his hands through the gravel of the path, looking for the right kinds of rocks. It was hard. Looking at tiny things made it clear he was seeing double. Closing one eye helped a little, but didn't fix it completely. He tried to reassure himself that the academy healer could fix it, but he wasn't entirely sure of that. Necessity forced him to put aside his fear. The forest was dim, and it would only get darker and more difficult to see as the sun set. Eventually, he found a small lump of quartz, a little smaller than the tip of his ring finger, though it was milky in color. He settled himself at the base of a tree and held the cloudy quartz in both hands, between his index fingers and his thumbs.

His crystal had been clear as glass, and it had grown evenly to a point. This stone was uneven and rounded, with traces of iron. He'd been given weeks to accustom himself to the way his mind fit with the crystal. He didn't have time to build such familiarity with this stone, but if he forced himself on it too quickly, it might shatter. He concentrated, pouring his energy into the quartz until it began to grow hot. Fearful he'd done too much, he cupped his hands around the glowing stone, waiting for it to crack. Miraculously, it didn't.

* * *

His night in the forest hadn't gone well. He was alive, but he was tired and grumpy. He was also extremely hungry. He'd grown up in a family of reasonable means, and his last four years had been spent at the academy where he ate well. Fasting was something he didn't do.

Hunting was out of the question; his eyes were better but still not right and he didn't have time. He did find a berry shrub and competed with the birds for his breakfast. Normally he would have used a finding spell if he'd been foolish enough to wander off without a snack. But last night's experiment with the quartz rock made him wary. He'd managed to cast the directional spell, but the instant it launched, he was overcome by a light so bright it blinded him. He'd lain on the forest floor, his head pounding, for what seemed like hours before he could see or even think again. It was small consolation that the spell worked. He'd successfully channeled his energy through the stone, and he'd gotten a definite direction.

He stomped down the forest path, carrying his cloak which was far too warm for his pace. He'd pulled some threads from the cloak to make a cord for his milky quartz stone. It didn't feel familiar, but it was better than nothing about his neck. He'd undone the top button of his black band-collar shirt, but he was still hot. He hadn't felt so uncomfortable since before he'd learned to use his magic, but at least he was making good time. He would point out to the masters that he'd made every effort to hurry back to the academy. If he was lucky he would be on the list to take the exam tomorrow or the next day. It was an academy tradition not to announce the testing order until the first day. If he was unlucky, he'd already missed his final. Anxious, he walked faster.

The sounds of chanting and shouting broke him out of his annoyed introspection. He caught a whiff of roasting meat, and his stomach twisted into a painful knot. Hopeful, he followed the smells and sounds. Surely there would be something for a lost stranger.

Over the next small rise and down a steep hill from the path, he found a great clearing. There were dozens of people wandering about, some busy with tasks, others apparently just visiting. A small group of children ran from one edge of the clearing to the other. He hesitated to approach. Something felt wrong, but as he hadn't mastered his quartz, he was unable to pinpoint what it was.

The chanting started up again, and his eyes were drawn to a small building on the other end of the clearing. A group of men slowly exited the building in a tight group. They appeared to have something or someone in their midst. He covered one eye so he could see more clearly. He scanned the clearing again, only then spotting the stake at the center. It was surrounded by a ring of kindling, and Rivel suddenly shivered, chilled to his very being. What kind of celebration *was* this? He dropped to a crouch and carefully moved toward some of the nearer trees. His hunger had been replaced with revulsion so strong he could barely master it.

The men had reached the stake, but they blocked Rivel's view as they tied up their victim. When they stood back, he could see it was a woman. What kind of monsters would burn a woman? He snaked his way through the trees to get a better look. He couldn't see her features clearly, but something made him decide she was young. He fancied she was pretty as well. Her hands were bound behind the stake, but she didn't appear uncomfortable. Several young children scurried to feed her from their plates. She spoke with them, and the macabre scene held some element of a Sunday picnic in the park. After the young woman was fed, the rest of the celebrants gathered around the roasting pit to eat as well. They sat in groups on the grass, scattered about the woman at the stake.

At one point a man stood and made a speech. His voice was quiet and he mumbled. Though he strained to hear, Rivel couldn't understand any of it. Afterward, everyone stood up and began cheering. The first man made a grand gesture, and another man approached with a burning brand. He bowed reverently to the woman tied to the stake before bending to light the kindling.

Horrified, Rivel mentally reached for his milky quartz and murmured a fire quenching spell. It was basic, and one of the first he'd been taught. It came off badly. The bright light of unfocused magic wasn't as overwhelming or painful this time, though it blurred his vision further. After a moment he could see that while he'd doused the roasting pit, the brand had only been reduced in intensity. Breathing deeply to concentrate, he cast a knot loosing spell. It was another simple spell, but it was poorly directed. Again, the light was less profound, but his head was starting to throb in time with his pulse. He'd thrown enough power into it to counteract his aim, and consequently untied every knot in the clearing. Men, women, and children hastily fastened garments and aprons that had suddenly come loose. The girl was unbound, but instead of running, she stood near the stake and looked about.

Certain she was paralyzed with fear, Rivel stepped out from behind his tree and waved urgently to her. "Run!" He shouted. "You're free! Quick! Run for your life!" He gestured toward himself.

The girl looked up and saw him, but made no move. He'd attracted the attention of others in the clearing, and they were pointing at him and shouting.

He was involved now and couldn't just leave her there, no matter how stupid and panicked she was. He pelted toward her. The first man who got in his way nearly tripped him up. Without losing too much momentum, Rivel managed to knock him over with an elbow to his chest. He grabbed the young woman's wrist, frankly surprised to have reached her first. Perhaps his appearance was enough of a surprise to buy him some time.

"Come on!" He tugged her behind him, slowing his pace to match her more reluctant stride.

"What are you doing?" she demanded, trying to pull her

arm free.

"Just trust me, I know what I'm doing." Three big men were gaining on them, and Rivel stopped and spun to face them, holding the young woman to his chest with one arm. "Stay back!" he cried, holding up his free hand. "I'm a mage, and I'll not hesitate to use my magic against you!" He conjured a wall of flame. It should have been easy. He'd mastered that spell two years ago for a midterm. Instead of a wall, he'd created a ring of fire around the clearing. He swore, and the girl twisted in his grasp to look up at him.

His adversaries initially appeared startled by the spell. After a moment they shrugged off their awe and began to approach more slowly.

"Keep back!" Rivel shouted, still holding his hand aloft in threat. The pain in his head picked up a more urgent tattoo.

"You can't take Karena from us," one of the men said. "She belongs here."

His mind grasped for his imperfect stone and he attempted one of his more complicated control spells. It was a poor choice. The explosion of the little building knocked him flat, sending the young woman off in a different direction. His eyes were tearing from the whiplash of power, and the three men reached him before he could regain his bearings. Years of bar fighting saved his life in those first few moments. He somehow managed to deflect the most dangerous of their blows. He was outnumbered at the start and it quickly became worse as others joined the fray. A low kick wrenched his ankle, and he stumbled to one knee. The circle of people around him grew tighter, more confining. The shouting and yelling was reduced to background noise and he couldn't make out individual words or threats. His hands were brought up behind his back as two of his attackers, big men from the feel of it, subdued him. He felt them draw the rope across his chest, tying his arms down and binding his hands tight behind him. When he struggled against the restraints, someone stomped on his calf. His mop of curly hair was grabbed from behind and he was forced to look skyward.

"What you have done is beyond profane," someone said

from behind him. He suspected it was the owner of the hand. "For that, you will die."

He watched the knife pass before his face, and gasped in terror as he realized what they meant to do. These were the last few moments of his life. A life that held little meaning or gain for anyone, himself included. There was some comfort in the fact that his last efforts had been spent trying to save someone else. Perhaps in the end it would be enough. As the blade settled on the left side of his neck, he closed his eyes, surrendering to the inevitable. At least it would be quick.

Magic washed over him, and his eyes opened in surprise. The knife disappeared. The grip on him was relaxed. He sensed the people were moving away from him, wandering off, but he couldn't quite bring himself to look. Faint with relief for his reprieve, he tipped onto his side, his hands still bound behind him.

After a while, he felt a pair of hands untying the rope, and he twisted to see the young woman he'd been trying to save. She met his eyes for a moment, but didn't speak as she continued working out the knots. Her hands were small, and her skin was the color of dried leaves. She was pretty. Her eyes were a shade darker than the chestnut hair that fell in waves over her shoulder. She wore a simple dress of undyed homespun wool and a brown leather vest. Around her neck hung a string of multicolored stones. If he were inclined to believe in the legends of fey folk, he'd suspect her of being one.

His hands came free, and he pushed himself to his knees to look at her again. "You're not hurt," he said in surprise.

"No. And you wouldn't have been, either, if you hadn't messed about in things you don't understand," she replied in a voice that flowed like silk. "What were you thinking?" she demanded. He was surprised so lovely a voice could deliver such a snap.

"I was trying to help you." He was stunned by her lack of appreciation.

She shook her head. "You're an idiot."

"They were going to burn you!"

She glared him into silence. "They do that every new

moon. Don't you know anything?"

He stared at her. "They burn someone every new moon?"

"No." Her voice was condescending, as if she couldn't credit his stupidity. "They burn *me* every new moon. It's part of my position."

His eyes slipped back to her necklace.

"That mob could have killed you," she said. "Would have if I hadn't stopped them."

"You're a mage," he whispered in awe. She'd been the source of the magic he'd felt. She'd sent his captors away.

"I'm a witch," she said firmly. "I don't need some silly perfect crystal to use my power." Her voice was full of scorn. She reached out and lifted the milky quartz from the base of his neck, holding it for a moment. "Did you lose your perfect crystal?"

He felt the heat rise in his cheeks. "It was stolen."

She grinned at him in a not altogether reassuring manner. "Quite a come down I imagine." She rose to her feet. "You must be pretty desperate to settle for that."

"To be entirely honest, I am." He lurched to his feet, wincing as his weight made his ankle hurt. "But if I don't get back to Trevia before my final exam, I may be expelled."

Her eyebrows arched slightly at that admission. "You're a naughty apprentice, are you?"

"I've had my share of trouble." It was all she needed to know.

She held out her hand. "I'm Karena."

He took her fingers in his own, and managed a somewhat clumsy bow, dropping a kiss on her knuckles. "Rivel Chamwell, M4 apprentice." He straightened up. "Truly delighted to meet you."

She smiled, appearing pleased. "I'll lead you back to Trevia. It's the least I can do, considering you were willing to die for me."

He smiled but couldn't quite bring himself to say something charming. It was still too soon after impending death for him to just shrug it off. He looked around. "What about..." The clearing was empty.

"They've gone home," she said as she hefted a bundle and stepped to the side he was favoring. "With the hazy memory of a fine celebration."

He swallowed his surprise. "You're strong."

She pulled his arm across her shoulders and wrapped her arm about his waist. "You can lean on me," she said as she gestured toward the woods.

He was grateful for her support as he gimped along beside her. "You can do all that with simple stones?" Perhaps her power was different, maybe she had a special talent for this.

"That and much more," she assured him. "The stones may be common, easy to find anywhere, but that doesn't diminish their power."

His eyes widened. If she was speaking the truth, and based on what she'd done he guessed she was, she could do far more than him. Did the masters have any idea how powerful this facet of magic was? If so, why did they refuse to teach it?

She looked up at him. "Like any magic, it takes practice. I suspect you could improve with time. And perhaps if you had a few friends for your lonely quartz. I rarely use only one stone."

* * *

"How do you use your stones?" Rivel asked. They had been walking for some time before he gathered the courage to ask. He'd never met a woman mage, or witch, since that was what she insisted she was. She was no mere apprentice.

"Much the same way you use your crystal, I imagine," she said. "You figured out how to use the quartz, didn't you?"

"Well, yes, but not nearly as effectively as I'd use my crystal."

"You're too dependent on a single tool, Rivel. All mages are." Her scorn was back. "It makes you much weaker than you need to be."

"It makes my magic very powerful," he countered. "I mean, a crystal is pure. No mage would think of using a flawed stone for focus."

"True enough. No mage would." She looked up at him, her expression unreadable. "But a witch would, could, and does.

I'm less vulnerable than you and your ilk. And while I prefer familiarity, I can use any stone." Her voice held a tone of pride. "There is more power in the common than you mages realize, and you're a pack of fools to ignore it."

"Our way is completely acceptable and effective..."

"Why use a single all-purpose stone," she asked quickly, interrupting, "when there are dozens of stones more suited to whatever spell you're trying to cast?" She shook her head. "Would you use a hammer when an axe would be more appropriate?"

"Of course not."

"It's the very same thing. You use the same tool for every spell, and a perfect quartz crystal isn't as suited to some tasks as other stones are." She shook her head again. "You deny yourself strength and power that is there for the taking. You're suppressing your gift. That's the worst part of it. You'll never be what you have the potential to be."

Her words made sense, but the accusation hurt. He'd used magic enough to know he was quite strong. He'd mastered his lessons at the academy with relatively little effort. Despite his wild tendencies it had always been his goal to be the best mage the academy had ever turned out. He'd assumed his natural abilities would bridge any knowledge or skill gap. He'd never considered he might be inhibiting himself even as he was learning to use his talent.

They continued their discussion of magic and aptitude as they walked. Rivel was unable to get her to share any actual spells, although she was willing, even eager, to discuss them in general. He suspected it had been a while since she'd been able to talk about magic with someone who understood.

It was growing dark when Karena suggested they stop for the night. "It's really not that far to Trevia," she said as she helped him to a downed tree. "You'd have made it back by now if it weren't for your ankle."

He'd been aware of their slow progress, but instead of feeling like a tedious trudge, it had been more of a pleasant stroll, the kind of activity one pursued when wooing a young lady. Although it had be chiefest on his mind that morning, he couldn't bring himself to be more than slightly concerned about the final he might have already missed. It may have been his brush with death, or even the blow to his head, but he doubted it. He was uneasy about the academy's lack of instruction in stone magic. He suddenly found himself hesitant to return at all. He couldn't explain the feeling and wondered if it was a reaction to the day's events. If he was being prophetic, he didn't really want to know.

"Just relax," she said. "I'll get a fire going, assuming you don't try to put it out this time."

* * *

Karena idly stirred the coals with her stick. In the dim glow she seemed more approachable.

"I haven't properly thanked you for your help," Rivel said, edging carefully toward her on their makeshift bench.

She looked at him, her eyes glinting back the orange of the dying embers. "You'd backed yourself into a corner, that's for certain. And how did you expect to get out of that situation yourself?" she demanded. "You're a helpless baby without your perfect crystal."

"That's how I was trained," he said with a shrug. "How was I to know there were other ways?" He wondered what her power would be like, given a perfect crystal. But then, perhaps she was right about stones being tuned for specific things. He wondered how she got a clear enough focus to cast the spells.

"There are always other ways." Her expression was bold, daring.

He smiled, "I guess there are." He moved a little closer. "And maybe after I've passed my exam I'll be free to research some of those other ways. The academy appears to have a gap in its curriculum."

She grunted. "Mages think their way is the best way. The right way. That's why your academy doesn't teach anything else."

"Just because they don't teach it doesn't mean we aren't willing learn it. You've seen what I can do..."

She laughed at him. "You're worse than the usual apprentice. What were you thinking, trying fancy big spells when you hadn't mastered the basics? I'm surprised you haven't killed your stone. It must be as stubborn as you are."

"Laugh all you like," he said with a grin. "I'm accustomed to big spells, and I pull them off routinely. Perhaps it's a bad habit," he admitted. "It's a lot more difficult to direct a spell through this." He fingered the milky quartz at his throat.

She grunted again. "Takes practice. And most M4 apprentices can't be bothered with such a trivial exercise as control."

"I'm bothering."

"Because you have no choice."

He met her eyes, refusing to be drawn into an argument. Even with her almost hostile attitude toward mages, he found her fascinating. He slid closer to her and bent his head to touch his lips to hers. He half expected her to slap him, or push him away, and he was fully willing to let her. Instead, her lips parted under his. Her fingers on his face and neck were gentle, loverly. He leaned back just slightly and brushed the side of her nose with his own before looking down into her face.

She suddenly pulled away from him and walked off, stopping beside a great old tree several lengths from the fire.

"Karena?" He rose clumsily to his feet. His ankle protested, and he ignored it. He limped toward her. "I'm sorry. I didn't mean to offend. I just... I like you. Rather a lot."

"Tomorrow you'll be back where you belong." He froze at the sound of her voice. "And you'll forget about me," she said firmly.

"I will not!" She was far too interesting to forget, and he didn't want to leave her. He'd never met anyone like her before.

She turned and glared at him, silencing him. "You're all the same, and you all forget. Or you don't care to begin with." She looked away from him and there was a long moment of silence. "I once thought that a night with a man like you was enough. But it's not."

He stared at her, a shadowy silhouette leaning against the tree.

"Go to sleep Rivel," she whispered. "Just... go to sleep."

* * *

He'd been awake for some time when Karena tapped him on the shoulder at dawn. She was silent as they ate a quick breakfast of roasted boar from the celebration he'd interrupted. "You should be home by noon," she said, placing herself beside him for support. "I hope that's soon enough for your exam."

"If not, it can't be helped," he said with a half shrug. His parents would be terribly disappointed if he were expelled, but even that wasn't enough to trouble him. The magus rating was no longer that important. In fact, he wasn't entirely certain he wanted to be associated with the academy. Realistically, he was powerful enough that he didn't need an official rank to make a living. He should have no trouble building up a reputation sufficient to support himself. Karena had made it clear there was more to learn than the academy taught, and he was suddenly very interested in that.

The edge of the forest was a short walk away, and as they stepped out into the unfiltered light of day, he could smell the salt and ash of the city. He blinked a few times, blinded by sunlight rather than magic, and he realized his headache was better. His vision was still blurred, though he thought it might be improved. Trevia was down a long gradual hill from where they stood, and he could see the peaked roof of the academy.

"We'll have to go carefully," she suggested. "You wouldn't want to go tumbling all the way home."

"Certainly not."

As they passed through the city gates she asked for directions. "Oh, I've been to Trevia," she assured him, when he expressed his surprise. "But what business would I have at your academy? I don't think your masters would approve of me."

He nodded his agreement. In the dim hours before dawn he'd considered the academy's prohibition of magic with common stones. The only logical motivation was political, and the thought that the academy stunted its students over something so pithy disgusted him. He'd nearly decided not to go back. But he realized he needed to make that decision based on fact, not an assumption.

"Let's rest a moment," he said. They stopped and he

relieved her of his weight. He immediately missed the touch of her body next to his. "I think I should go the rest of the way alone."

"You can't walk on that ankle."

"Karena, I really appreciate your help." He paused. How much detail did she need? "The masters must be furious with me by now. I've caused them enough trouble already."

"Have you then?" She had a wicked gleam in her eye. "You're that waggish?"

"They've only kept me because of my talent," he admitted. "And returning like this is gong to be difficult to explain. If you come with me, they're going to want to talk to you. And they aren't exactly even-tempered individuals."

She wrinkled her nose. "Oooh. Musty old mages."

"I mean it," he said, squeezing her shoulder for emphasis. "They're going to interrogate you, and you don't deserve that."

"I understand. I'd expected it. I'd seriously doubt the credentials of a school that would let you disappear for days, return injured, and not question the entire business." She smiled. "At least I won't have to lie when they ask if you've seduced me."

Startled, he stared at her, a half-formed protest on his lips.

"I'm taking you home, Rivel." She gave him a last stern look. "It's the least I can do. When you thought I was in danger, you risked your life to save me. And your masters should know that you acted in goodwill. They should know that you were delayed by injuries sustained in the attempt to save a life."

He felt the tingle of the visitor detection spell as they crossed the academy's threshold. It would only be a moment before someone came.

He ran his hand across her back, putting his arm around her shoulders. He gave her a gentle squeeze, and she looked up at him. "I'd like to see you again."

"You just want my secrets." This time, there was no venom in her voice.

He shook his head. "I'd like you to teach me, if you'd be willing. Maybe we can trade," he suggested. "But I don't want this to be goodbye." She wrapped her arms around him, and he returned the embrace. He was still holding her when the master on duty arrived.

* * *

Rivel woke in the infirmary. A wave of unease washed over him, and he stiffly pushed himself up. He was alone, and the midmorning sun was shining through the window. He reached to his neck, where an unfamiliar crystal hung on a silver chain. He gasped at the shock of being parted from his quartz stone, and for a moment his chest hurt. It was worse than losing his first crystal, but then, he couldn't really remember that. He forced himself to relax and breathe normally.

There was nothing on the small table beside the bed. A pile of clean clothes sat on a nearby chair. They'd taken his things; his quartz and the green stone Karena had given him before she left. She'd told him it was good for finding. He kicked off his blankets and pawed through the clothes. They were spares from his room in the dormitory.

"So you're finally awake."

Rivel spun toward the door, at the sound of the voice. Master Greyfels, the academy healer stood in the doorway, smiling. His expression wavered slightly. He closed the distance between them in three strides and pushed Rivel back onto the bed.

"You look a bit pale to be up yet," he said. He pressed one hand to Rivel's forehead and frowned. "How do you feel?"

"Like something's wrong." Rivel rubbed at his head with both hands. It didn't hurt, and his eyes were fine now, but he felt unbalanced.

Greyfels peered into Rivel's eyes a moment and nodded. "It's the new crystal," he said gently. "I've fixed the knock to your head, but you talented ones have a more difficult time adjusting to a new crystal. It'll pass."

Rivel nodded and touched the crystal again. It hadn't accepted him yet.

"As soon as you feel up to it, the masters would like you to take your final," Greyfels said. "Nearly everyone else is done."

"I'm ready," Rivel said. He wanted it over. Once he had his rank he'd be permitted to ask the questions he needed answered.

60

"You're sure?"

Rivel nodded.

The healer shrugged. "Very well. You may return to your room. Someone will come for you when the masters are ready." He stepped out of the way to let Rivel retrieve his clothes. "I suggest you spend your time getting to know your new crystal," he said before leaving the room.

* * *

Rivel silently followed the second-year student through the halls. He'd spent the last two hours lying on his bed and working with his new crystal. It was his now, but it still felt stale and cold. His ankle was just beginning to ache when his guide stopped at a door. He'd never tested in this room, but his previous tests had all been minor in comparison. The door opened, and Rivel entered alone. The masters were seated on one side of a great table, facing him. Headmaster Tennerly made a beckoning gesture and pointed to the lone chair opposite the masters.

Rivel crossed the room and nervously settled himself on the chair.

"How's your ankle?" Tennerly asked gently.

Rivel met the headmaster's eyes, not trusting his tone. "Better, headmaster."

Tennerly smiled. "And your new crystal? Have you had time to accustom yourself to it?"

Rivel nodded.

"You've completed your time at the academy, and have excelled in your lessons, despite yourself." His face was expressionless. "Usually we require a demonstration of magical ability, but your previous course work makes a practical exam unnecessary to the point of absurdity."

Rivel stared at the headmaster. "You're going to graduate me without an exam?"

"You're a very talented young man, you know," Tennerly said. "However, before we can confer you with the title of magus, there's something we need to discuss."

Rivel glanced at the other masters, suddenly doubting that they regularly attended finals, even those for graduation, in so

61

large a group. Something was definitely wrong.

Tennerly held out his right hand, and the master on that side of him placed a small velvet pouch in the headmaster's palm. "Do you know what's in here?" he asked in a whisper.

"No," Rivel lied.

Tennerly opened the pouch and spilled two small stones onto the table.

"Those are mine." Rivel met the headmaster's eyes. They'd been confiscated, then, not merely misplaced.

"When you returned yesterday, you were wearing this." Tennerly's finger pointed to the quartz. "You'd been using it to work magic."

Rivel didn't answer. There was no need to. One only had to feel the stone to know it was his. He was unsure how he'd bonded with it so quickly, but it seemed to be calling him.

"A magus uses a perfect crystal, Rivel. Common magic is forbidden in our order."

"Why?" Rivel demanded. He wanted to snatch his stones away from the headmaster but didn't dare. Not yet.

"It's impure."

"It's powerful," Rivel insisted. "We're limiting ourselves by relying on one tool."

"The crystal is the tool of a magus, Rivel. Common stones are not." Tennerly's voice was even, almost calm. "And this is what I was afraid of."

Rivel glared at the headmaster, refusing to comment.

"You've been contaminated by your contact with this obscene kind of magic," Tennerly said. He held out his left hand. The master on that side draped a long cord over his wrist. The headmaster gently placed it on the table, well away from the stones. "You know what this is?"

Rivel nodded. It was the token of a magus. The thin black and purple ropes were wound tightly together, and crowned with a tassel on each end.

"As I mentioned earlier, you're very strong," Tennerly said. "We would prefer to keep you in our company. We are willing to overlook your transgressions. The decision is yours."

Rivel scowled at the headmaster. They would forgive him if he chose the cords over the stones. He could leave the room with one or the other, not both. He'd spent years grooming himself for the duties of a magus. He'd met men wearing the badge with pride, and envied them. Now he could only pity them.

He got to his feet and snatched up the stones. He registered the headmaster's surprise and stalked out. They hadn't expected him to make this decision. They thought to bribe him back.

"You're a failure!" Tennerly shouted. "You'll have no where to go now!"

Rivel looked down at the green stone in his hand and smiled. How wrong they were.

The Jezic Box

Caleo's fingers tightened on the boat's cold metal railing as she leaned forward and looked out over the sea. She'd never seen so much water at one time. It was fabulous.

She'd been thrilled when she qualified for the Denbrick summer program in advanced magic. Only the best students in the nation were invited to spend August on the Denbrick island estate.

Her granddad, who'd come along as a chaperone, was suddenly beside her. "It's windy out here," he said. "Why don't we go back inside?"

She rolled her eyes. "You can go in, if you want," she suggested. She grinned when he made a disagreeable noise. The wind *was* blowing hard, and she was glad she'd tied a scarf over her head. Her short curly hair was hard enough to keep in check in the gentlest environments. "So are you ready to tell me why you came along on a high school field trip?"

"You *know* why," he said sourly.

"Humor me."

"Your dad thinks you spend too much time with that one

over there." With three fingers, he pointed emphatically to the other side the boat.

Jennan was sitting near the opposite railing, puzzling over a notebook, as usual. His gold wire-rimmed glasses were crooked, but he didn't seem to notice. He lived across the street from Caleo, and they'd been friends since third-grade.

"If it weren't for him, I doubt I'd be here," she said. "He's always been better at instant magic than me, and he's helped me a lot." Jennan chose that moment to look up, so she smiled and waved. He nodded once, then turned back to his notebook. His soft blond hair was blowing and tangling in the wind, and she wondered if he'd forgotten to tie it back. She was fond of the notion that he was a genius; he got so distracted by his own thoughts that he forgot about everything else. He was constantly sketching and building things. He'd told her that every spell, every piece of magic, had a shape. If he could figure out the shape, it helped him understand how the magic worked. Most people brushed off his geometric theories as absurd, but she knew better.

"You're going to follow the family pattern, if you're not careful." Granddad looked at her and shook his head. "You're too young."

She laughed out loud. "I'm seventeen. I'm already older than mom was when she met dad." She gave him a wicked smile, her round cheeks dimpling and mischief glinting in her blue eyes. "And didn't you marry grandmum when you were seventeen?"

"That was different. I was going off to war," he said. "I thought I was going to get killed by one of those western sorcerers."

"You worry too much," she said. "I don't think Jen's even discovered girls yet." She patted her granddad's hand and left him there. Jennan was sitting alone as he worked, poking at the page with his stylus. She sat down and considered his sketch. It looked inside out. "What's that?" Most people used special formulae to build spells, but Jennan started with the shape, which he could design around the purpose. Caleo had found his way faster and more accurate.

"It's something new I'm trying out," he said. He grabbed

65

the lines with his stylus and moved them around. He changed the shading from red to pink, absently nodding his head.

"What does it do?" He'd taught her to see the shapes of spells, which improved her spell crafting so much that she was one of the best in school. She'd been on last year's varsity craft team, and she'd placed ninth at the individual level in the nationals.

"So far, nothing." He sounded disgusted. "I'm doing something wrong."

"But what's it *supposed* to do?" She tilted her head and examined the design again. "Does it have to do with dreams?"

He looked at her, surprised. "What makes you say that?"

She giggled. "Are you trying to mess with someone's dreams, Jen?"

Two spots of color came up in his cheeks, and he quickly closed the notebook. "No."

He was saved from further interrogation by an explosion of excitement at the bow. Students were rushing to the rail. Caleo was too polite to shove through the crowd, but she was too short see over it. She stood up on the bench. It was as if the island had sneaked up on them, or just appeared out of the water. It was no mere speck far off in the distance. She couldn't see the veil of magic that must have hidden it.

"We're almost there!" As she jumped off the bench, she bumped Jennan's hand, and his notebook went flying. He grabbed for it, but missed, and it fell overboard. Instantly creating a spell to suit the moment, she caught the notebook before it could hit the water, and returned it to Jennan's hand. "Sorry."

"That's all right." He'd rarely gotten angry with her, no matter how many of his designs she'd accidentally damaged. He shrank the notebook and tucked it into his pocket. "Nice catch."

Places cleared at the railing as students hurried into the cabin, eager to be first off. "Come on," she said, grabbing Jennan by the arm. "Let's watch from up here." He didn't resist as she propelled him to the railing, where they could see the boat docking.

A large building of light pink stone stood in the middle of the island. At the center, over the main entrance, was a gigantic five pointed star in stained glass. It reached from the second floor to the fourth, and it was the grandest thing she'd ever seen. Across the front of the building, smaller stars of clear glass caught the sun. The mansion was four stories tall, plus the attic, but the steep gray roof made it seem much taller. A golden railing enclosed a widow's walk at the top. The attic's tiny star windows peeked out of evenly spaced dormers. In front of the mansion, and wrapping around the right side, was a large expanse of green lawn dotted with decorative shrubs and trees. Off to the left was a thick woods, which looked wonderfully creepy.

Something out of the corner of her eye made her look at the mansion again. One of the attic windows glowed silver. Jennan was leaning over the rail, trying to see the docking mechanisms. "Hey Jen, do you see..." There was a strangled cry behind her, and she spun in time to see her granddad collapse. "Granddad!" She was beside him without realizing she'd even moved. His skin was hot, something he couldn't tolerate for long, and there was a prickly feeling of magic in the air. She doused them both with several gallons of cold water and slapped at his cheeks. He was trying to work a spell, but he was too weak. She reached out with her mind and felt for the shape. It was columnar and blue. With that as her guide, she cast it for him. He glared up at her, breathing easy again.

"What do you think you're doing?" he demanded, his voice low. "That's *not* a spell you should try without training."

"Are you okay?" she asked, ignoring the reprimand. Her hair was plastered to her head, and her clothes were soggy.

He nodded, letting her help him to his feet. He looked surprised when he noticed Jennan on his other side, ready to assist. "I'm fine," he insisted, brushing off the young man's help.

"What was that?" Caleo asked. "There was a light and magic."

"It was nothing," her granddad snapped. "Now just let me alone."

Alerted by one of the students, a woman wearing a healer's badge suddenly appeared on the deck. She strode directly toward Caleo and her granddad.

"There was no light," granddad whispered to Caleo, his voice firm. "No magic."

She knew better than to question him when he used that tone. She had the impression that he didn't expect her to believe him, just that he didn't want to talk about it.

* * *

Caleo was deep into the orange team's territory when someone tripped her. She tucked tightly and rolled, then hopped back to her feet facing the orange team captain. He was much taller than she. The cheering and screaming from the sidelines was muted, as if it were happening far away. The coaches were still shouting orders to members of both teams, but Caleo wasn't listening.

She let him make the first move. While many people liked to start out offensive, she found that playing defensively gave her a better chance to measure her opponent. Using a bit of flight, she jumped out of the way of his stunning spell. He definitely led with his right side. She grinned and sent confusion at his right, immediately following with a sleep enchantment at his left. He countered the confusion, but wasn't ready for the enchantment. It hit him full on, and he dropped to the ground.

She took a moment to assess her team, letting her psychic awareness catch the details she couldn't see. Her own captain, Polly, was on the other side of the field, and Caleo wondered why the tall gangly girl hadn't given the signal yet. Then again, she suspected most of the students didn't realize what the Connection spell did. Polly broke free of her own opponent and sent up a blue fireball. Caleo cast her portion and, as she'd expected, found herself part of a greater consciousness. As her power and skill merged with her team mates', she felt stronger than ever.

Despite having been the first team to successfully cast the new spell, they nearly lost the match anyway. Terrified by the results, two members of the blue team became more of a hindrance than a help. Their minds gibbered fearfully against the others. Again, Caleo was struck by Polly's slow response. She reminded herself that speed was her own specialty. Not even Jennan could keep pace with her.

Every student was assigned to lead their team for one match. The Denbrick instructors insisted that it was as important to be able to follow a designated captain as it was to provide good leadership. Since they spent so much time on it, Caleo figured the lesson must be pretty important.

Polly guided the blue team through disabling the rest of their opponents, and at the whistle Caleo released herself from the spell. The sun was too bright, and her hearing returned with a roar. She squinted a little as she looked around. She and her nine teammates were standing in the center of the field, alone.

"Woo hoo!" She raised her arms above her head and did a little victory dance. "That was so cool." The two who'd responded poorly to the spell, still looked pale. "Are you all right?"

"Did someone tell you what it was going to do?" Tim asked. "No one warned me." He sounded irritated, as though he were convinced he'd been left out.

Caleo shook her head. "I guessed."

"I'm not a wimp," Susan insisted. She'd immediately become popular among the other students, but she didn't seem to have much confidence in her abilities. "My training has always been very strict, so I'm used to being better prepared."

"You did fine," Caleo said. "You cast the spell perfectly."

"The match goes to the blue team!" A loud voice boomed across the field. "Blue team receives points for defeating the orange team, for successfully casting the Connection spell, and for using it as an essential part of the operation. Blue team leads with three points."

Caleo smiled as she exchanged shoulder taps with the rest of her team. "Good job," she said as her two fingers touched the back of Polly's shoulder.

The taller girl let out huge sigh. "I'm just glad I'm done being captain. That was hard."

"You may proceed to your afternoon activities," the announcer said. "Classes will resume at three o'clock."

Caleo was looking for Jennan when she felt a hand on her shoulder. She turned and found herself face to face with the young man she'd knocked out on the field. "Oh, hi," she said.

"Hi," he said. "I don't think we've met. I'm Garryn."

"I'm Caleo," she said.

"I know. I asked around. My friends are already teasing me about the way you nailed me. They think it's really funny." He smiled and shrugged, looking a bit embarrassed. "You don't look like you can spar the way you do."

"Thanks. I *think*," she said. She wasn't entirely certain if that was a compliment or not. Guys frequently didn't say quite what they intended around her. Their brains seemed to scramble when she talked to them. It was best if she used as few words as possible.

"How'd you do it?" he asked.

"I just move fast," she said. "You might also practice throwing spells off the left side."

"Ah." He smiled stupidly at her and kept nodding his head in little bobs. She hated it when guys went all vacant like that.

With his usual sense of timing, Jennan appeared and stepped between her and Garryn, as if he hadn't noticed she was speaking to someone. "I've been looking all over for you," he said, brandishing his notebook. "You've got to see this." He looked up, apparently noticing Garryn for the first time. "Oh, excuse me. Are you busy?"

She barely managed to keep her composure. She somehow doubted he could possibly be *that* oblivious. "I think we're done." She waved to the glassy-eyed Garryn. "It was nice to meet you." Then she followed Jennan away. "Thanks," she murmured.

He grinned down at her. "No big. Looked like your charm hit him pretty hard, and I know how you love that."

He *had* noticed. "What have you got there?" she asked, trying to get a look at his notebook. It was closed, so he hadn't wanted anyone else to see.

"That Connection spell," he said. "When you guys got it to work, I was able to see its shape." He looked at her again. "Did you know what it was going to do?"

"I'd guessed." They had reached the back garden of the mansion. Perfectly maintained stone pathways meandered between the flowerbeds. The blossoms complimented each other

70

in color, shape, and scent. Trees and shrubs had been trimmed to look like animals or interesting shapes, and she idly wondered what spells might share similar designs. They walked until they reached a large fountain with three stone mermaids sitting back to back and playing flutes. Water poured out of the ends of their musical instruments, and small ornamental fish swam around the sirens' submerged tail fins. Caleo snorted.

"What?" Jennan asked. He glanced up the statues. "Don't you like them?"

"They don't look anything like real mermaids," she said.

"And you would know?" he asked. He looked at her as if she were a spell that he was trying to figure out.

"Actually, yes." She didn't want to talk about it just now, so she reached for his notebook. "Aren't you going to show me what you found?"

He sat down on the wide flat edge of the fountain and leafed through to a page in the back. "Here." He held it out to her. "Tell me what you see."

She took the notebook and sat beside him. The spell was three-dimensional, which meant he was probably itching to build a model of it. His father hadn't let him bring any of his materials, insisting that he needed to learn to focus on the real world. The spell's base was spherical, and there were several conical points sticking out of it. The central part was lavender, and the points were much darker. She used his stylus to make it rotate on the page. There were ten points in all, and they weren't equal in size or shading. Some were small and pale, while others were bold purple. On one side of the sphere there was a strange indent, and on the opposite side there was a bulge that she strongly suspected was the reverse of the indent. She glanced at him, puzzled, then turned back to the slowly moving shape on the page.

"Well, there are ten people on my team, and there are ten points on the spell, so I suppose each of those might signify one of us," she said slowly. He never laughed at her, even when her guesses were very different from his own, and sometimes she figured out things that he hadn't. "It reminds me of a pop bead."

"What's a pop bead?" he asked.

71

"Little kids make jewelry out of them. I used to have tons of them," she explained. "Each one has a peg on one side and a little hole on the other. They snap together, so you can make a chain as long or as short as you want."

"So what does the spell do?" he asked, in the voice he always used when he already knew.

She took a deep breath. "It combined all our strengths and abilities. I think that if we'd all been working together better, we could've been incredibly powerful."

He nodded. "Okay, what else?"

She stared at the design.

"Think about the pop beads," he suggested.

"Oh!" She suddenly realized what he was saying. "Several groups could cast the Connection spell, and then lock together with each other to be even stronger. And they'd be less vulnerable, because they'd be in separate groups."

He beamed at her.

* * *

"Is this about right?" Jennan asked handing her his notebook.

Caleo glanced at the thin blue cylinder on the page, and nodded. It was the spell she'd cast during her granddad's strange attack on the boat. He still refused to talk about it and insisted she'd been imagining things, but he wouldn't meet her eyes when he said it. "I thought it might be some sort of counter. That's what it felt like."

"It is." He glanced around, but they were still alone, walking the path through the back garden. "It's a *serious* counter."

She looked up at him. He'd felt the magic too. "What do you mean?"

Jennan emphasized the distance between the top and bottom of the column. "Most counter spells are shorter here. Whatever you were blocking had to be really big, or really bad. Either way, it was very powerful."

It confirmed her suspicions, but only made her feel worse.

"You're really good, Cal," he said. "That was a tricky spell to cast, and you did it without ever seeing it before."

She shrugged. "I couldn't have done it if I hadn't seen the shape." She considered asking why anyone would want to kill her granddad. She was convinced the spell she'd blocked wasn't intended simply to hurt him. They walked into a paved square with a statue in the middle. Her granddad stood in front of the statue with his head bowed, as if he were reading the plaque. He was rubbing at his nose the way he did when he was upset. "Granddad?"

"Aren't you supposed to be in class?" His voice was rough.

She shook her head and walked over to him. "We have free time right now." She was relieved to notice that Jennan had tucked away his notebook. Granddad would get unreasonable if he knew what they'd been working on. The statute was a woman wearing military dress, and she had several medals hanging on the front of her uniform. "Did you know her?"

He nodded. "Sammy was the last of the Denbricks."

"Did she die in the war?" she asked gently. Granddad didn't like to talk about the war. He wouldn't even tell her what his job had been. She'd gotten the impression that he'd been involved with something very bad, and most of his friends hadn't survived.

"No." There was such anger in his voice that she inadvertently took a half step away from him. "She was murdered, like the rest of her family." He turned on his heel and walked away.

Caleo looked down at the brass plaque in between Samantha Denbrick's feet. During the Vision Crystal War, she'd served with the Elite Fifty-Three. She'd been instrumental in ending the use of the barbaric Jezic Box, only to have her family systematically hunted down by Emile Jezic. The rest of the plaque continued with information on the wonderful things Samantha and the other Denbricks had done. Like many powerful families they were well respected for their contributions to society. This was all well and good, but not terribly helpful.

"Who were the Elite Fifty-Three?" Caleo asked.

"They were special squad during the war," Jennan replied. "Reconnaissance and interrogation, I think."

"What's a Jezic Box?" She'd heard of it before, but couldn't place it.

"It's a torture spell," he said. "It traps you inside a magical box with a tangible representation of whatever you fear most. If your worst fear is psychological, it uses symbolism, like dreams do. They *say* it's unblockable, but that's impossible."

"How do you know all that?" It sounded very nasty, and she was a little disturbed to think that Jennan had been a researching it.

"I've seen it mentioned, so I looked it up. Jezic never told anyone how it works. He's the only one who ever cast it." He gave her a small smile. "I don't think I can figure it out without seeing it, or at least spending a lot more time on it than I have."

"Are you sure?"

He nodded. "I'm not interested in torture spells, Cal, honest. Now come on, I want to try the Connection spell with you." Together they'd adjusted it so they could cast it with just the two of them. They'd lack the power of multiples, but would be stronger than they were individually.

Altering spells with Jennan was one of her favorite hobbies. Despite what their parents or instructors might think, neither of them were rash, and they were very careful when they tested something new. She smiled. "All right."

* * *

Caleo rolled over and looked across the darkened room she shared with fourteen other young women. None of them were snoring, or talking, or making any appreciable noise. She felt completely awake, which was ridiculous because it was the middle of the night, and the last few weeks had been a lot of work. She got out of bed, thinking a walk might remind her body that it was supposed to be sleeping.

She stood in front of the window and raised her arms over her head in a stretch. Her eyes caught movement, and she froze. Who else was up at this hour, and what were they doing out in the garden? She dropped her arms and inched closer to the window. Under the dim glow of the moon, she recognized her granddad. He was walking as if he was going someplace specific, and that was too peculiar to ignore. She shoved her bare feet into her shoes.

When she peeked out the window again, granddad had reached the woods.

She wished she were better at blinking, which would have brought her to the garden in an instant. She'd only learned the spell recently and wasn't really comfortable with it. If she used it without concentrating hard enough she could end up half where she planned and half where she'd started. She left the room quietly, ran down the spiral stairs, and out into the yard. She enhanced her vision for night and found a path into the woods. It was obviously not a frequently used path, and her overlong t-shirt caught on several shrubs. Her steps were slow, and she looked all around as she moved among the trees. She half expected something to jump out at her.

She paused when she heard voices. They were too far away to tell what they were saying. She crept forward until she could hear. She paused, identifying two voices, then continued until she could see. She crouched behind a leafy shrub and watched. Granddad and another man stood just off the path, arguing.

"... even if all the others believed you were dead, I wasn't convinced," granddad said.

"They should have known better," the other man said, as if agreeing. For some reason, his voice reminded her of the slimy scum from the top of a stagnant pond. "Why, the Fifty-Three themselves had a motto about these things."

"I'm quite familiar with it," granddad snapped.

"But you're the only one who believed in it," the other man said. "You've never given up." His bitterness was almost palpable. "Unfortunately, I can't appreciate the sentiment. Your refusal to believe that I was dead has simply made my life more difficult."

Caleo cautiously separated the shrub's branches to get a better look. The stranger's gray-streaked black hair was pulled into a short ponytail. He had deep dark eyes, much too small for his face. His thin scraggly beard did little to hide the sharp angle of his chin.

"Spare me your sob story, Jezic. I've had it with you," her

granddad said. Without warning, he threw a spell that Caleo had never seen. The shape was unfamiliar, though it felt sharply pointed at one end, and she was certain it was designed to kill.

Jezic blocked it as if he'd been expecting it. "Now, now, Theo," he said. "You always did have a temper."

"At least I'm still human," granddad snapped. "I don't think you ever were."

"You don't want to make me angry," Jezic said. He sounded so much like a grade school bully, and if the situation hadn't been so critical she might have thought it was funny. "I haven't gotten to use my spell in a while, and you might say I'm anxious to find someone to experiment on. I've made some improvements during my exile."

"Aren't you special," granddad said. "I always knew you were a one-trick-wonder. You're no genius. You just happened upon one powerful idea that you were able to make work. In forty-six years you haven't developed a single new spell. That's... well, it's pathetic."

Jezic scowled at granddad. "Pathetic, is it?" he asked.

"Yeah," granddad said. "But that's what you've been your whole life. Too scared to face someone in a fair fight. Sneaking about and resorting to surprise attacks. Even Sammy expected better of you. She defended you. Thought you'd just gone astray. And you killed her."

"Like I'll kill you." Jezic snapped. "You've always talked too much, Theo."

As Jezic was raising his hand to cast a spell, Caleo's granddad turned his head and happened to meet her eyes through the shrubbery. His mouth dropped open in surprise and his expression turned to horror. She didn't see exactly what happened next, but she thought he might have tried to cast several spells at the same time, a sure way to fail at casting any of them. There was a blinding flash of light and she was thrown backward. She got up in time to see Jezic breaking through the underbrush toward the mansion. Her granddad was on his knees, and all the trees in the area were singed.

"Granddad?" she whispered, inching out from behind the

bush.

"Get out of here," he said quietly. His voice was harsh, and he was clutching his head as if it hurt. "He may be back, and I *don't* want you here if that happens."

She touched his shoulder. He was weak, but otherwise okay. "I can't leave you."

"Caleo Fuxa..." his voice was stern.

"No." She helped him to his feet. "What's going on?"

He glared at her. "No one's ever succeeded in hunting down that bastard and I *have* to make sure he doesn't get away this time. He's hurt too many people." He stood on his own, wobbling a bit.

"Why you?"

"Calie, it's not safe here. Get to the house, and take the back way."

Normally that tone would have gotten instant obedience, but Caleo was too worried about him to listen. He wasn't in any condition to go after a crazy sorcerer. Deciding quickly, she spun and sprinted down the path the direction Jezic had gone. She ignored her granddad's shouts, knowing he was too weary to catch up with her. At the edge of the woods, she looked around. She didn't know what she'd do if she found Jezic, but she'd worry about that when she got to it. Out of breath, she ran up the small hill of the front lawn, where she had a good view. Jezic came crashing out of the woods nearby, swearing and yelling. Despite his apparent disorientation, he noticed her, and in an instant he was next to her on the little hill. She considered blinking, but Jen's warnings had been impressive.

"You're Theo Fuxa's granddaughter, aren't you?" he demanded. "I've been keeping an eye on him, and you for that matter."

She tried to hit him with the same series the spells she'd used on Garryn during the blue team's first match. Jezic blocked them, as well as the next three she cast in quick succession.

"Kid stuff," he said. "I think Theo will be quite crushed to find you in one of my boxes. And that's all I really want. Once his spirit is broken, I'll kill him."

That made her angry, but he didn't give her time for a response. She felt something pressing against her mind, rapidly followed by magic she'd never experienced. She saw a series of shapes, then she was in a cramped wooden crate filled with lobsters easily half her size. They snapped at her with their claws, but she was too furious to be scared. "No!" Jezic wanted to hurt her granddad by hurting her. She wasn't about to let that happen. She pushed against the top of the crate, and it disintegrated, spilling large irritated lobsters all over the yard around her. Jezic stared at her, his expression a mixture of shock and fear.

"You won't shut me up in your stupid box!" she shouted. She cast the killing spell her granddad had thrown at Jezic earlier, but he blinked out.

"Calie! Calie, are you okay?" Granddad ran up the small hill toward her. He halted just out of reach of the lobsters.

"Don't tell me you're afraid of lobsters too?" she demanded, still angry although her target was gone.

"They're not my favorite," he admitted. He lifted her away from the shards of the crate and the scurrying snapping crustaceans. "Are you okay?"

"I'm mad, but I'm fine," she said.

"What did you do?" He held her at arm's length and stared at her. "How did you get out? No one's ever done that before."

"I don't know," she admitted. She needed some time to think. She badly wanted to talk with Jennan. He was better at sketching than she was, and he might be able to help her sort out what had happened. "Now what was that all about?" she demanded. "And I want a real answer."

He looked away. "That was Emile Jezic."

"I'd figured that out." She crossed her arms and gave him as stern a look as she could.

He let out a huge sigh. "He was my friend... once. But I guess he was always warped. When Sammy got after him about his spell, he snapped. He killed her whole family, and a lot of my friends in the process. I have to catch him Calie. I owe it to Sammy and the others."

"You *can't* do this yourself," she said, horrified that might be what he was planning.

"I have to. You wouldn't understand." He turned toward the front door. "You belong in bed, and we're not talking about this again. Clear?"

"As an oligotrophic lake."

* * *

Caleo groaned as she stared at her sketch. "This isn't turning out at all," she complained. "I wish you'd been there. Then *you* could draw it." They were sitting on the edge of the mermaid fountain in the bright afternoon sun. She'd always appreciated Jen's special talents, but she was beginning to wonder if she'd been taking him for granted. She wasn't new to magic or his theories. Why was this so hard?

"Can you tell me anything more about it?" he asked.

She shook her head. Granddad had forbidden her to tell anyone, but she needed Jennan's help, and she couldn't hide this from him. "It happened so quickly." She was about to tear out the page and crumple it up, as she had with every other attempt, but he stopped her.

"Wait a second." His hand caught hers, at the edge of the page, reinforcing the command. He squinted at her drawing. "Are you sure it was only *one* spell?" he asked. "It looks like you're combining at least two shapes."

"You think so?"

Glancing at her picture as he worked, his stylus moved rapidly over a page in his own notebook. "I think... you have one... like this." He'd finished a small rough outline on the top half of the page and started on another on the lower half. "And another... a little like... this." He held his sketches next to hers for comparison. "What do you think?"

She stared at his designs, then closed her eyes and concentrated on the seconds just before she'd found herself in the Jezic Box. There had been a moment when she felt pressure against her mind. She opened her eyes and looked at Jennan's notebook. The shape on the bottom half of the page bore similarities to the Connection spell they'd cast as a team. It was likely in the same class, although it clearly did something very different.

She turned to a blank page and started a new sketch, using Jennan's as a model. She'd seen the shape at the time Jezic cast the spell, but he'd followed it up so rapidly with the second, that she'd squashed them together as one. She now understood why no one else could cast a Jezic Box, and why it had proven unblockable. It wasn't one spell, but two that worked together. Blocking one would be enough for the spell to fail. That or being faster than Jezic in casting it.

In two dimensions, it looked like a figure eight. In three, it was two connected spheres, barely overlapping. One was gray, lighter toward the back, and darker where it touched the other. She started making the second sphere red, but that didn't feel right. Color was very important when dealing with a graphic representation of a spell. She ended up making it bright orange, with dark streaks across it instead of gradual shading.

"Wow," Jennan said. "That's a nasty piece of work."

She didn't need his guidance to figure out what it did. "It's weak here." She tapped the place where the two spheres merged. It was an odd mix of gray and orange. "It's not a one-way connection. He touched my mind to find what I was most afraid of. In that moment, we were on equal ground. I just didn't realize it."

"And it's not a basic mind touch spell," Jennan said. "This is far more complicated."

"What would you know about that kind of spell, Jen?" she asked.

"I've read about them. They're relatively simple, and they take alteration fairly well," he said, looking flustered. "This one finds the fear. That way he only has to touch his victim's mind briefly, limiting the amount of time he's vulnerable."

She turned the page and started on the second design. "So now we know how he discovers what you're afraid of," Caleo said. "This part must be the box itself."

"It's a little convoluted to be a box," he said.

She giggled. It was another one of those lopsided inside-out looking spells

80

"Were you scared?" he asked.

"I was more angry than anything," she admitted. "He wanted to use me to get to my granddad." She rotated the spell and continued to work on it. "I guess I was frightened too. You know what the Jezic Box does."

"More than anything else, you're afraid of lobsters?" he asked. "Or were they symbolic?"

"They weren't regular lobsters," she said. Normal lobsters were no big deal. They could be reasoned with. "They were giant sea lobsters. Have you ever seen the pinchers on those things?"

"But why lobsters?" he asked. "Why not bears, or saber tooth mountain goats?"

She looked at him. "Fear is absolutely personal. Nobody is the same. And fear doesn't necessarily make sense. What's your greatest fear?" She was annoyed with him. He was interrupting her work on the spell, and she felt stupid about the lobsters. "I bet I could cast this first part. Should we find out what you're afraid of, so you can explain it to me?"

"Please don't."

She immediately regretted threatening him, and looked back down at her notebook.

"I'm sorry," he said quietly. "You're right about fear, and I shouldn't tease you."

"That's all right," she said. "And I wouldn't do that spell on you. You know that, don't you?" She looked at him again.

He nodded. "Cal, are you a mermaid?" he asked suddenly.

She stared at him, startled. "My great-grandmother came from the sea," she said, unwilling to lie to him.

He nodded, as if he'd suspected for some time. "Is that why most guys can't put two sentences together around you?"

"Yes."

"Why doesn't it affect me?"

"You're special," she said.

"If that means I can like you, and still talk to you, then I guess that's okay," he said. He took her hand. "Do you like me?"

"Of course I do," she said.

He shook his head. "I don't mean as a friend."

She leaned over to kiss him and didn't have to stretch as much as she'd expected, because he met her halfway. He kissed well, and she was suddenly jealous that he might have learned with someone else. She'd wanted to be first. Then again, kissing wasn't exactly complicated.

He looked down at her. "Your parents don't like me," he said.

"You'd noticed?" she asked.

His lips twitched and he smiled. "I just pretend to be self-absorbed. I thought you knew that." He slipped his arms around her. "Is that going to be a problem, your parents?"

She shook her head. "They're just afraid we'll elope before graduation."

"What?"

She shrugged. "Sirens tend to pair off young," she explained. "My mom and dad finished school and went to college, but they also eloped when they were sixteen."

"Do we *have* to get married?" he asked, sounding a little worried. "My dad doesn't think I've even discovered girls yet." He rolled his eyes. "And that might blow his mind. Literally." He tangled his fingers in her curls and she wondered where he'd put their notebooks.

"I don't think there's any reason to rush," she said. "Just because a lot of mermaids marry young doesn't mean I'm going to." She let him hold her for a moment more before forcing herself back to work. "Now help me with this spell. I really need to understand it."

He frowned. "You want to use it on him, don't you?"

Her ears burned and she looked down. She should have known he'd figure out what she had in mind. Jezic's spell had failed on her granddad, probably because some of his random magic blocked one of the components of the box. Then she'd broken free of it. If she were Jezic, she'd want to prove it still worked. "He's still here. And he's going to go after me or granddad." Her granddad was still exhausted when she'd seen him that morning. He'd been lucky twice, because she'd been there. She didn't think he could survive another confrontation with Jezic.

"It had better be me."

* * *

Caleo was anxious. She'd never been so torn about something in her life. She wanted to find Emile Jezic and see if she was right about his awful spell, but at the same time she hoped he'd vanished, never to return again. She kept speeding her pace, only to be held back by Jennan's hand holding hers. Finally, he stopped walking and pulled her to him.

"What's the hurry?" he asked. "This is supposed to be a moonlight walk."

"I know. It's just..." she shrugged, unable to articulate exactly what she was feeling.

"You don't actually think he's hiding somewhere you could find him, do you?" he asked in a whisper. "If he's here, he's probably watching you now. But he'll wait until he thinks the moment is right." He tipped her chin up and smiled at her. "He can't have this moment. It's mine." He kissed her then, forestalling any argument on her part. "Now let's walk for a while, and pretend that's why we're out here."

"Why pretend?"

He laughed. "Fine. We'll pretend it's the *only* reason we're out here."

They wandered through the well groomed garden for quite some time. When they reached the fountain, Jennan looked at the three mermaids and cast a curious glance at her.

"What?" she asked feeling self-conscious.

"Do you have fins?" he asked.

She shrugged. "Sometimes."

"What happens when you sing?"

Feeling mischievous, she leaned toward him and hummed the first part of a tune she'd known all her life. It was a delight to watch his reaction. His eyes widened and he took on a much more intent expression. His mouth opened slightly, and a hard shiver ran through him.

"That's what happens." She kept her voice soft.

"Wow." He smiled. "You'll have to do that again some time, when we're alone."

83

"I'd like that."

It was time. Jezic wouldn't come after her unless she was by herself, and she needed to be his target. Jennan pulled her close for a moment. Then he whispered in her ear, "Keep your head, and you'll be fine. I'll be watching you. Stay angry."

"You remember granddad's spell?" After they'd dissected the Jezic Box, she'd showed him the deadly sharp-ended spell from the previous night.

"I don't forget shapes," he reminded her. "See that you don't either." He stepped back, looking reluctant, and vanished.

He hadn't been gone a full minute, when the space he'd vacated was taken by a much older man. His dark little eyes expressed anger and hate. "Out for a romantic stroll, are we?"

She jumped, startled.

"And does Theo know where his little granddaughter is?" Jezic leered at her.

"My boyfriend will be right back," she said, hoping it sounded like a threat.

"Oh, has he gone to get something?" he asked with a wink. "Such a naughty girl you are. You will have to be punished."

She felt the sensation of his spell touching her mind again, and she thought very hard about the shape of the spell. On top of it all, she concentrated on speed. In the very instant she knew his greatest fear, she cast the second half of the spell, finishing mere seconds before he would have. She actually felt his magical box forming around her before it was abruptly cut off. She stood, panting and sweating, in front of a large wooden crate. She knew it wasn't really wood. That was just how it manifested.

Jennan reappeared. "That was close," he said. "It's a good thing you're so damn fast."

"Do you think he'll realize how to break it?" she asked. The yard lights came on, and she heard noise from inside the mansion. The reinforcements Jen called would be out soon.

He shook his head. "I doubt it. *We're* not even sure of that part." He'd suggested that the Jezic Box was a self-reinforcing spell. The victim's fear fed the magic. Because she had been more angry than scared, the box had failed.

"Calie!" Her name echoed across the estate. Granddad blinked into the garden and stared at the box, then at her. "Calie?"

"I'm fine," she said. A horrible wail started from inside the box. "Though I can't say the same for him."

Granddad gawked at her. "Is that... did you...?"

"She trapped Emile Jezic in his own box," Jennan said. He squeezed her hand. "I saw the whole thing."

She watched her granddad's eyes slide from their clasped hands to Jennan's face before he looked at her, his expression accusing. "What were you doing out here? And with him?"

"I was waiting for Jezic to show up again," she said. "I thought I could trap him."

"That's not why I was here," Jennan said. He grinned impishly down at her.

Her granddad swore quietly. "Your parents are going to kill me," he muttered. A group of people dressed in military uniforms came charging into the garden, and he glared at Caleo one last time before turning to speak with them.

"I guess there's still one of the Elite Fifty-Three around," Jennan said. "Did you know?"

She shook her head. "Not until last night." She looked up at him. "Have any more shapes you want to share?"

In the Shadow of Altai

Sarangerel's thoughts were as heavy as the rugs lining her grandparents' yurt. Summer was usually her favorite time of year; it meant moving from the dull desert plains to lusher, greener parts of Altay Prefecture. They'd established their first summer camp yesterday, with Shaman Munkhjargal blessing it last night. Normally Sarangerel would be at her happiest, but this year was different. Uncertainty weighed heavily on her mind.

Over her shoulder, she carried a pole with a pair of nested buckets swinging on the end. She heard the babble of the river before it came into sight. Pausing, she closed her eyes and let herself be one with the sound. The river had the right of it. It traveled from high in the Altai Mountains, through the prefecture, past transhumant and permanent villages until it reached the lake south of Altay City. There, it met up with the water of other rivers. She, too, yearned to travel, not just this seasonal migration, following the best grazing for their livestock. As she'd grown, her people's claim that they were descended from the Great Altai Wolf began to feel artificial. She wanted to move with purpose, like a true wolf, not this aimless wandering of her ancestors. Whenever the subject came up, she and Grandmother would argue while Grandfather sat on his cushion looking disapproving. It was unfair that his simple expression held such power. She'd never dared ask if he'd used it on her father when he was a child or her mother once they'd married. And some ghosts did not speak.

Running her fingers across her forehead, she banished thoughts of the dead. She tucked loose hairs behind her ears; they were too short to stay in the thick black braid down her back. At seventeen, she had long since put aside the paired braids of a girl. This winter, she had even taken up a headscarf when the desert winds became a nuisance. Galchinua had teased her, saying she looked like somebody's wife. There'd been a hint of a smile on his face and a special glint in his dark eyes. That memory lifted her heart, and she continued on her way.

The trees were greener and thicker near the river. The roots of some looked like they had jumped out of the ground to reach over the bank to the water. This late in the morning, the river was quiet and clear. The goats and camels had been watered hours ago before being driven into open fields of new grass. Her first duty was to fetch water, then she'd be back with the laundry. Sarangerel would gladly spend the day here. As she filled her second bucket, she heard the sound of rocks sliding together underfoot, letting her know she wasn't alone. She turned.

Galchinua smiled sheepishly. "You never let me sneak up on you."

"You are not to be trusted." Since no one was there to witness her boldness, she grinned.

He laughed, as open and free a sound as the river. "I was beginning to think you weren't going to make it."

"I promised I would," she said, serious now. "I wouldn't break my word, not to you."

"I didn't mean it like that." He stepped closer, but didn't touch her as he took both buckets, lifting them with ease. He set them farther up the gradual rocky slope. "I just know you aren't as free as I am."

That was an understatement. He'd been a treasured boy

child, the only one of his mother's offspring to survive more than a year. He nearly always got his way, though somehow he hadn't become spoiled or overbearing. It wasn't his nature. "Aren't you supposed to be fishing?" It was half the reason she'd volunteered to fetch the water and do the laundry.

He nodded, then pushed back his straight, chin-length hair. "I've caught several already." He stared into her eyes for a moment before turning coy. "Shall I bring some to your grandmother this afternoon?"

As usual, his flirting made her giddy. "You know she'll ask you to dinner."

"And it would be rude not to accept," he replied. He placed his right hand in the middle of his chest, his brown fingers splayed over the dark blue fabric. "I am never rude."

She raised one eyebrow. "Never?"

"Hardly ever," he amended with a shrug. "But perhaps you will forgive me for being young and impetuous."

"You're surely both," she agreed. Though his seventeenth birthday had not yet passed, he was able to get away with behaving as a man for the most part. No one chastised him for stepping out of his place. Sarangerel laid her staff over her shoulders. "Grandmother is waiting for the water. But I'll be back." Holding the staff across her shoulders, she bent and caught the handle of one bucket with the end. Turning and squatting slightly, she deftly caught the second bucket on the other end.

"Hurry," Galchinua suggested. "I fear I may pine while you're away."

She felt the heat of a blush in her cheeks and looked down, only a little ashamed to lose control of her emotions in front of him. It was hardly the first time. It also helped that she'd been able to get under his skin a time or two. She gave him a little bow, then turned to the path.

* * *

"More tea, Grandfather?" Sarangerel asked, rising on her knees as she lifted the stout metal teapot. Settled people used ceramic instead of tin and steel. They could afford the luxury of fragile things that wouldn't survive a wandering lifestyle. At

Grandfather's slow nod, she poured tea into the cup across from her own. "Galchinua?" She turned toward him, sitting to her left at the little square table.

"Yes please." He briefly met her eyes before looking across to her grandmother. "Thank you for the lovely meal, Grandmother." He bowed his head. "It was delicious, as always."

"The credit goes to you, Galchinua," Grandmother replied. "Your fish were very fine."

"They may have been fine," he agreed. "But without your skills they would have remained simply fish."

"I understand you're on watch this evening," Grandfather said, cradling his warm cup in his hand.

Galchinua nodded. "My father and I both."

"We should take care we don't make you late," the old man replied.

"Are you trying to send me away, Grandfather?" Galchinua asked, voicing Sarangerel's suspicion.

Grandfather let out a snort and shook his head. "Hardly. You'd only come back anyway."

"True," Galchinua agreed. Sarangerel knew he was relieved, and hoped it was just that she knew him so well, not because it was obvious. "I'll finish my tea and be on my way."

She hadn't known about his watch duty and was disappointed. He managed to get himself invited to dinner frequently, and they usually went walking afterward. Watch was more important. Their livelihood depended on keeping their stock safe. Though there hadn't been an attack by human or animal in longer than anyone could remember, the watch was taken as seriously as if it fought off marauding Huns on a regular basis.

Sarangerel gathered up the dishes and carried them outside to the washbasin, leaving Galchinua and her grandfather to chat. She was drying the last of the bamboo plates when Grandmother joined her.

"Your boy is growing up," Grandmother said, the approval clear in her voice. "Going out with the watch is no small thing." She shook her head. "Most don't serve on the night watch before their initiation."

Sarangerel shrugged. "Galchinua isn't going through the initiation."

"He'll change his mind," Grandmother said.

Sarangerel turned to her grandmother, annoyed. "You always say that. What makes you so sure?" Did she pay no attention to the boy who came so often to dinner? Did she understand him so little? "He's not one for rash decisions, and when he makes up his mind, not even an earthquake will move him."

Grandmother grunted, unimpressed. "I've seen that side of him, yes. But he can be swayed by reason. Once he sees what it does to you, he'll understand better. He is a true son of Altai, and he'll want her power for himself."

Sarangerel held back a shiver. They didn't speak much of the initiation, and when they did, it sounded mystical, even frightening. "What power?"

Grandmother shook her head again. "I can't tell you more than I have. It's forbidden." It was the response such questions always brought.

Sarangerel clenched her teeth for a moment. Only children lost their temper, and she was no child. "What if I decide not to do it?" she asked. She'd been considering that option since Galchinua told her his plan. Once they were both of age, they could travel to a village or even a city. They were smart and strong; they'd find work easily. There was no need to bind themselves to the wolf as their ancestors had. She realized Grandmother was staring at her. "Well?"

"Did Galchinua put you up to this?" her grandmother demanded, her voice low and quiet.

Sarangerel straightened up to her full height. "He didn't need to. I have my own dreams. I want to make something of myself and do important things."

"So this life isn't important?" Grandmother asked. She waved a hand around at the widely spread yurts. "The way of the people you were born to, the people who raised you aren't important? What would be important, Sarangerel? Cooking all day for those who don't know you and don't care what happens to you? Washing the laundry of strangers? What could be more important than living in time with the earth as we are meant to? What could be more important than understanding your purpose in life?"

She'd intended to make Grandmother back off, not to suggest that their way of life was completely meaningless. Sarangerel stared at the brown felted wool of their yurt, sure she'd cry if she looked up. "I don't feel like my purpose is to be the wife of a shepherd," she mumbled.

Grandmother took a deep breath. "You're a child of Altai. There is power and knowledge for you here. You can only claim your birthright through the initiation. If you forgo that," she hesitated, as if it was difficult for her to say this. "If you do, you will be hollow. Like our Chinese and Siberian kin who've lost their way. You'll never find your purpose. And you will doom your descendents to lives without meaning."

Sarangerel felt a cold chill race up her back. Grandmother's words sounded like fact, premonition.

"I'm not saying you have to abandon your dreams." Grandmother turned to pile the plates and chopsticks together. "I just ask that you go through the initiation. Afterward, you may do as you wish."

Until now, Sarangerel had the impression she had to choose one or the other. Perhaps there was a trick. "You won't try to make me stay if I decide to leave?"

"We will not try to make you stay if you don't wish it," Grandmother promised. "I just want you to have all we can give you before you make that decision. And you wouldn't be the first of our people to go."

"I didn't know that," Sarangerel said. No one spoke of those who had left. They talked plenty of the dead, the ancestors, and the Great Altai Wolf.

"There's much you don't know," Grandmother said, her voice gentle. "Until midwinter, you were a girl, and you're still young for all that you're now a woman."

"I'll go through the initiation," Sarangerel agreed. It meant so much to her grandmother, it was the least she could do. Her grandparents had raised her after her parents were gone; she couldn't ignore their wishes completely. "But I still don't think Galchinua will."

Grandmother sighed, looking relieved. "It's unwise to count your lambs before midsummer. Galchinua won't risk losing you to someone who has accepted his birthright."

Sarangerel still had her doubts, but she didn't voice them. She'd never noticed a change among those who'd gone through the initiation. Then again, she hadn't known any of them well. A high fever had run through the clan the year before she was born, causing a gap in children. She was the first born after the fever to survive, and there were five in her age group. Three had come of age in the spring, and the others would join them later this summer.

* * *

Sarangerel and Galchinua sat back-to-back on a large flat stone that hung out over the river. Thin wispy clouds concealed what little moonlight there was, and the stars were bright pinpoints in a blue-black sky. He'd turned off the small solar-powered lamp Grandfather insisted they take, claiming he didn't want to run the batteries down.

"My initiation's on the next full moon," she said, after taking several minutes to build up her courage.

"I'd heard," he said.

"You had?" she asked in surprise. Was he disappointed?

She felt his shoulders move as he shrugged. "I think everybody knows by now, but Batuldzii told me a few days ago." Batuldzii was Shaman Munkhjargal's son, and in training to be shaman himself one day. He was also Galchinua's best friend, though he was nearly three years older.

"Are you mad at me?" she asked, locking her fingers together and wrapping them around one knee as she looked up at the sky without seeing.

His hair brushed against her neck as he moved his head. "No. It's your decision to make. Though I thought you might skip it."

Relieved, she took a slow breath. He always challenged her to think for herself, and she wanted to make sure he knew she had, especially with this decision. "It means so much to my grandparents, and it's only one night." She shook her head. "I can do that much for them. It's not going to change my plans. And they've promised they won't try to make me stay, after."

"They really said that?" It was his turn to be surprised. "Do you believe them?" He sounded curious, not doubtful.

"Yes." She answered both his questions. "Grandmother told me others have left."

"Of course they have," he said, as if everyone knew it.

"But not all of them have married into other clans," she explained. "Some have gone to find a different way of life."

"I know," he said, and she wondered how he'd known what she hadn't. "I just didn't expect your grandparents to be open to it, not after the way your father went."

Sarangerel twisted to look at him, laying one hand on his shoulder. "What do you mean?"

His hand slipped over the top of hers as he turned his head to meet her eyes. "You do know what happened to your father, right?" His voice was cautious.

She shook her head. "After Mama died, he just... vanished. One day he was gone." She'd been young, almost four. The first night Baba hadn't come home, she didn't even notice. He'd been odd since her mother's death, and he often went out with the night watch. It was only after several nights, when she saw the significant looks between her grandparents, that she asked.

"He left," Galchinua said softly.

She shook her head. "He couldn't have. He took nothing with him."

"I'm sorry. I thought you knew." He turned to face her completely, his big hands curving around her shoulders. "Some say he killed himself, but his body was never found, and people looked in all the likely places. If he told your grandparents where he was going, they've never said. I heard he was strong, that he probably went south to work in construction."

Sarangerel looked into the river. She could only see occasional glimpses of starlight on the tips of the waves. The rest was simply moving darkness. Why hadn't her grandparents told her? That was a stupid question. What would you tell a four-year-old? The truth hurt, but it would have been worse to grow up knowing that her father had left her behind. It made sense, really. She'd been too young to be much use to him; she would have slowed him down and made it difficult for him to find work. And what would a widower know of caring for a child? Leaving her with his parents was the kindest thing he could have done.

Galchinua's voice brought her back to the moment. "Sarangerel?" he sang her name more than spoke it, gentle and coaxing. His fingertips brushed her cheek, something he never would've dared do when others might see.

Turning to him pressed her face more firmly against his hand, but he didn't pull away and neither did she.

"Where did you go, my Moonbeam?" he whispered.

"It doesn't matter," she said. "I'm here now." She reached out, pausing briefly to remind herself that he was only sixteen and she had no right to touch him this way. Then her hand was on the warm skin of his neck, his pulse beating against her palm.

He let out a sigh, and she felt his breath across her face. He bent and kissed her, just the briefest brush of his lips against hers, before straightening up.

Gasping in shock, she pulled back.

"I'm sorry," he said quietly, looking meek. "I shouldn't have done that."

"If I'd known you were going to, I wouldn't have let you." She doubted her own words, but had to say it. "I mustn't take advantage of you."

His wide smile was barely visible in the dark. "I don't feel like I'm still a boy when I'm with you." The unusually low pitch of his voice made her shiver in a pleasant way.

"It doesn't matter how you feel," she said, as much to herself as to him. "We can't do things like that until after your birthday. If people found out..." she shook her head. "They would say I tempted you. I'd be dishonored."

"I wouldn't let anyone say that about you," he insisted, though he didn't move any closer.

"You wouldn't have any control over it. You know how

people are." Though he wasn't an adult, he was less than six months younger, and he'd seen enough human behavior to know she was right. "If I'm dishonored, our plans will be ruined."

He bowed his head, signifying she had won the debate. "I intend to marry you, Sarangerel." It was the first time he'd stated it so directly. Normally their discussions were stated as hypothetical possibilities or couched in euphemism. "I haven't worked so hard to gain your grandparents' favor just to mess it up in the end."

She wanted to dance around with joy, and it was no small feat to keep the emotion bottled up. "We should get back. I just wanted to tell you about the initiation. She turned on the lantern, low so it wouldn't blind them. "I'm sorry you had to hear about it from Batuldzii."

He shrugged. "I guess I understand."

"Which part?" she asked. "The fact that I'm doing the initiation, or that I didn't tell you right away?"

"The second." He glanced toward the path before looking directly into her face. "I'll be honest, I don't know why you're going through the initiation. It's your choice, but I can't see what good it will do. Why bind yourself to the Great Altai Wolf? It's just going to make people think you'll stay."

She didn't answer right away. She was afraid he thought she'd given in too easily and chose her words carefully. "There are really two reasons."

He resettled himself beside to her, obviously prepared to hear everything she had to say. He folded his hands together and gazed at his fingers, making it easier for her to speak. Sometimes words didn't want to come when he was boldly looking into her eyes.

"My grandparents have done so much for me," she explained. Though she didn't want to continue their way of life, she loved them and knew she would miss them when she left. "They've cared for me as though they were my parents."

"They're your family, Sarangerel," he said, unimpressed. "They're supposed to do that."

She shook her head. "It's what our people expect, but they didn't have to. Not all grandparents would have." Again, they had both seen enough in their travels to know she spoke the truth. "I'm grateful for what they've done. And I mean that, it's not just words." She'd heard people say so many things they didn't mean, she'd learned to trust actions more. "I love them. It will cost me nothing to do this. It won't delay my plans."

"Our plans," he corrected.

"Our plans," she agreed, allowing herself a small smile. "It's the best way to show them I appreciate what they've done."

"That's a good enough reason on its own." He was quiet for a moment, his expression thoughtful. "Do you think it's selfish that I don't intend to show my parents the same respect?" He stayed completely still, and she sensed tension, almost nervousness. It was strange. He was normally so confident.

She shook her head. "I don't judge you, Galchinua. My reasons are not yours." Though they didn't always agree, one of the things she'd always liked about him was that they could have their own opinions. While they might discuss them, she never felt pressure to change hers to match his. She wasn't sure how she felt about him not going through the initiation, but she didn't want to talk him into anything he was opposed to.

He nodded, still silent and contemplative. "You said there were two reasons," he finally said. "What's the other one?"

She was less comfortable sharing this part. It sounded like superstitious silliness. "Promise you won't laugh."

"Why would I laugh?" he asked, surprised.

She shrugged and looked at the river, mostly to avoid meeting his eyes. "This is harder to explain. A little less solid."

"The way you feel about something can be very important in the decisions you make," he said. "So if that's what it is, I won't laugh."

"It is." How did he always know what to say to help her explain herself? She thought he might be that way with other people as well, though she hadn't seen it as strongly. "I'm a little scared," she admitted, her voice barely audible over the river's.

"Of the initiation?" he asked.

She shook her head. There was no such thing as failure. "Of not doing it." She took a deep breath, continuing before he could ask anything that might distract her from her point. "I'm afraid if I don't do it, if I don't acknowledge the link to our ancestors and the Great Altai Wolf, I'll lose something forever. It's like there's a part of me that's empty, and it will stay that way. If that happens, my life will never have meaning. I'll be like the Mongolians who lost all ties to their clans and no longer even know who they are." Awkwardly holding the lamp, she wrapped her arms around herself to ward off the chill, but it didn't work. This coldness came from inside.

"I don't think there's a part of you that's empty," he whispered. "And I know you well." She turned toward him, but he held up a hand to keep her from interrupting. "But if you feel this way, you should do the initiation. You even have my blessing, if you need it or want it."

"You mean that?" she asked, hearing the surprise in her own voice.

He smiled. "I do. This way, you won't later question whether you should have done it."

"You don't think I'm being silly?" The ancestors knew she'd accused herself of that often enough. In the morning, when the sun was brightest, her fears seemed foolish. But at night when she lay in the darkness, they seemed more real than her blankets or the pallet beneath her.

"There's magic in this world. It's not just a thing in our tales," Galchinua said. "If you feel this way, there could be good reason. This may be something you need to do." He shrugged. "I don't have the same feeling, so perhaps what's right for you isn't right for me."

She felt as though a weight had been lifted from her heart. Although they'd always managed to come to some sort of agreement, she worried this time would be different. She could enjoy the spring now. Her initiation would happen, making her grandparents happy, but not disappointing Galchinua. Then she only had to wait for his birthday.

* * *

Sarangerel walked beside her grandmother in a long line following Shaman Munkhjargal and Batuldzii. She was used to hiking, sometimes for days on end, but today she was curious about their destination in a way she usually wasn't. "Where are we going?" she asked, as they passed the men herding the goats for the day.

"To the steppes," Grandmother said. "It's about fifteen kilometers to a place where we can see both the Altai Mountains and the Celestial Wolf."

It was about a four-hour walk, and it would be dark soon after they reached their destination. "Won't the moon make it difficult to see the Celestial Wolf?"

Grandmother shook her head. "Not for us."

The afternoon wore on in pleasant conversation. About a quarter of their clan had come along, and there was a festive atmosphere. Eventually, the three initiates drifted together. First Delgernandjil caught up with Sarangerel. They were such close friends that most people referred to them as sisters.

"I'm nervous," Delgernandjil said quietly.

"I'm not," Sarangerel said, a little surprised by that truth. "I guess I'm glad it's finally come. I was more worried before."

Delgernandjil raised one eyebrow. "When you had to explain yourself to Galchinua?"

Sarangerel grinned back. "It went very well."

"I thought he'd talk you out of it," Delgernandjil admitted.

"He didn't even try."

"Who didn't try what?" Temurvachir asked, appearing at Sarangerel's other side. He was strangely tall for their people, towering over Sarangerel, and he was built like a bear, all muscle.

"Galchinua didn't try to talk her out of the initiation," Delgernandjil said.

"You're a nosy one" Sarangerel said, reaching up to lightly slap the back of his head.

Temurvachir laughed out loud, drawing looks of disapproval from those around them. As his name suggested, he was a thunderbolt, quick to respond with anger or joy. "You don't know him very well if you thought he'd try," he said to Delgernandjil. "If he wants to change your mind, convince you of something, he doesn't use words. He doesn't need them."

"Grandmother calls it presence," Sarangerel said. It was what made Galchinua a natural leader. His words and actions carried weight and made people think about their own.

"He'll keep you on your toes, that's for sure," Temurvachir said.

"Me?" Sarangerel asked innocently.

Temurvachir rolled his eyes. "As if we don't all know he's courting you."

"Is that what he's doing?" Sarangerel asked, feigning surprise. "I thought he was just a sweet boy who liked visiting my grandfather."

Delgernandjil hid her smile behind a hand.

Temurvachir tried to look disapproving, but the twitching of his lips gave him away. "He is but a boy, yet. If he's being a nuisance, I can send him back to his mother for you," he offered.

Sarangerel shook her head, declining politely. "You are so kind. But I think I have the matter well in hand."

"Just let me know if you change your mind," he said. "You're like a sister to me."

"That's so sweet," Delgernandjil said.

"He may not have meant it as a compliment," Sarangerel said, eying him.

He laughed again. "Like an older sister, I can never pull one over on you."

The rest of the afternoon passed quickly. When they reached the wind-bent grasses of the steppes, Shaman Munkhjargal stopped next to the last tree. She beckoned to the initiates, and Sarangerel obediently went to her. The shaman gave each of them a handful of ribbons. Sarangerel's were red, Temurvachir's were green, and Delgernandjil's were yellow. The clan members took one ribbon from each of the initiates, tying them to the lower branches of the tree. While prayers had been tied into other trees on her behalf in the past, Sarangerel was certain there had never been so many all at once. The kindness was unexpectedly touching, even if it was simply ritual. She silently traded ribbons with her friends before adding her sincere best wishes for them.

After the last ribbon had been tied, Batuldzii led them into the steppes. Here, the wind could be just as strong as the desert's, though Sarangerel found it less harsh. This evening, there was only a light breeze. It had been present all day, keeping her just comfortable on their long walk. The temperature would drop a bit with the sun, but it should be a mild night. The sky was clear, which also seemed a good sign. Initiations happened even if there was rain.

When everyone else stopped, setting down their baskets and bundles, Sarangerel glanced at her friends. Though the place looked no different than any other part of the steppes, they had obviously reached their destination.

Shaman Munkhjargal and Batuldzii were seated with her grandparents when Sarangerel reached them. The shaman and her son wore matching ceremonial tunics, sheepskin dyed turmeric yellow. Small beads of wood and bone the color of tea leaves made outlines of wolves. A large one raced across Batuldzii's back, and a smaller one stood with its head tilted up to howl on the right side of his chest. A thick bushy tail ran down the shaman's left arm. Red and brown thread stitched the shapes of paw prints and the moon.

"Good evening Shaman," Sarangerel said, taking a place between her grandmother and Galchinua's best friend.

"It's very good indeed." Her face was perfectly round, and she only had a hint of age creases at the corners of her eyes. "I'm glad you decided to join us tonight."

Sarangerel looked at her grandmother, wondering if she'd told the shaman that she'd considered forgoing the initiation, but she saw nothing in Grandmother's expression to support the question. "It seemed the wisest course of action."

Shaman Munkhjargal nodded in agreement. "Perhaps you will be able to persuade young Galchinua to see it in the same light."

Sarangerel shook her head. "I'm sorry, I can't do that." From the corner of her eye, she saw Grandfather stiffen. "If he goes through the initiation, it must be his own choice."

Although he didn't smile, something in Batuldzii's expression was reassuring. "You're right of course," he said. She wondered if he'd tried to convince his friend or if he would accept whatever decision Galchinua made. "We weren't asking you to try to change his mind."

Sarangerel relaxed. There was no doubt Galchinua could be valuable to their people, and she fully expected them to try to get him to stay once he was of age.

"Each of us is our own person," Batuldzii said. "And Galchinua is more so than most. But he isn't afraid to change his mind; he doesn't see it as a weakness. If you hadn't come tonight, I'd fear we'd lose him forever." His smile was small, appropriate in a social setting outside the family, but it spoke of his relief. "You've given me hope that he could yet see the wisdom in following this tradition."

"The future isn't written in stone," Sarangerel allowed, though it still seemed unlikely.

"It never is," Shaman Munkhjargal agreed. "And if we remember that, particularly at our most difficult times, we can see there's always cause for hope."

Before Sarangerel had finished her dumplings, Batuldzii bowed to each of them, then stood up. He slipped the felt cover off his drum, wrapping his long fingers around the wooden cross piece on the back. He slowly wandered through the group, his thumb tapping a slow beat.

Shaman Munkhjargal met her eyes, holding them. "And so it begins."

"What's going to happen?" Sarangerel asked. Surely there was no longer any need for secrecy. The initiation was underway; there would be no escaping it.

The shaman grinned, showing crooked teeth that were still white. "Patience. Time will reveal all." She rose to join her son. Her song started low, barely audible above the gentle breeze, and Sarangerel couldn't catch the words, much less the meaning. The sun was dropping beyond the steppes as she helped her grandmother gather their things and put them aside with everyone else's. Apparently dancing would be part of the ceremony.

Since nothing significant seemed to be happening, she let herself think about Galchinua and their plans. In a few weeks, he would turn seventeen. Following proper protocol, it would be a few more weeks before they could marry, so it would probably be early fall before they left. It was a good time to travel, but they still had to decide where to go. They'd discussed trying a larger village first, to get used to living with so many people in a fixed location, but Sarangerel suspected there would be more jobs, and they'd be easier to come by, in the city.

The sound of Batuldzii's drum right behind her, louder than it had been before, pulled her back to her initiation. The full moon hung low on the horizon, and the first winking dots of starlight began to appear in the sky opposite it. Those who knew what was going on had moved to form a line facing the Altai Mountains. Sarangerel found her place between her grandparents.

Shaman Munkhjargal sang of their ancestor, praising her and calling her down to her people. As the darkness began to rise up, Batuldzii's voice joined his mother's. Sarangerel heard him sing at other events, but not as often as his mother. As happened on those occasions, she was struck by the beauty and clarity of each of his notes.

The song was long, and at some point Sarangerel lost track of it as her eyes caught sight of a brighter light in the sky, barely visible above Altai's peaks. She touched her grandmother's shoulder, but didn't look away, afraid it would fade.

"I told you we'd have no trouble seeing the Celestial Wolf tonight," Grandmother whispered, sounding a little smug.

As the song continued, the star grew brighter, unnaturally so, making it clear magic was afoot. The light shone down in a single bright ray, arching over the mountains and reaching toward the steppes. Not a ray, Sarangerel realized, but a bridge stretching from the Celestial Wolf to them. She was gratified that Delgernandjil and Temurvachir looked equally amazed.

The song ended as the bridge of light touched the ground in front of Batuldzii. The silence was strangely deafening, as if Sarangerel's ears weren't quite working. She wanted to approach the bridge, touch it and see if it was real, but she didn't dare. No one else had gone forward, and even Batuldzii and Shaman Munkhjargal stood with quiet respect, one on either side of the ribbon of starlight.

Temurvachir's gasp caught Sarangerel's attention. He stared farther up the bridge, toward its start at the Celestial Wolf. Something or someone was crossing the span. She was difficult to look at, glowing as brightly as the bridge she walked, and though Sarangerel couldn't see well enough to make such a distinction, she felt certain it was a female. When the being's feet finally reached the grass of the steppes, her brightness faded slightly. She was no longer blinding, but seeing her better made her form no more clear. She was a wolf, yet she was also a woman. From moment to moment, step to step, she seemed to change from one to the other. Wolf. She bowed to both Batuldzii and Shaman Munkhjargal. Woman. She straightened up and looked out at the assembled line, seeming to breathe deeply through her nose. Turning slightly she walked directly toward Sarangerel.

Wolf. Woman. Wolf. Woman. Sarangerel's eyes watered from the brilliance and sight of two creatures inhabiting the same place at the same time. She bowed when the Great Altai Wolf stopped in front of her.

"Give me your hand, child." The voice was in her head, gentle but firm. "I have a gift to bestow upon my Moonbeam."

Uncertain, Sarangerel held out her right hand. It was taken by glowing fingers that felt warm and smooth yet insubstantial. Altai turned Sarangerel's palm to the sky. Wolf again. A damp nose brushed against Sarangerel's skin, the soft muzzle hairs and longer whiskers tickling. A tongue as wet and as real as a lamb's, but also as solid as smoke, brushed over her palm, making it tingle. The sensation spread down her arm and through her whole body, making her tremble as though she were cold. She felt a snap in her chest, as if something had been made right or complete inside her. Without needing to ask, Sarangerel knew Altai had given her wisdom, something that normally came only with age, and not everyone acquired it.

Woman. Altai met Sarangerel's eyes. Her glowing form smiled, then bowed, shifting again to the wolf. She walked slowly down the line, stopping next at Temurvachir. To him went the gift of hunting, which Sarangerel realized applied well beyond a life

103

within their clan. True, he could stay and protect their people, providing them with wild game as a break from mutton. But he could also go out into the world, making a very good detective or spy. Delgernandjil's gift was agility. Although Sarangerel would have once found that useless to woman of her people, she now understood better. Agility could keep her from getting hurt as she worked with restless herds. But it would also allow her to move with the elegance of an acrobat or dancer. Her friends shivered as she did, while the magic made its way through their bodies.

If she looked carefully, Sarangerel could see the gifts of the others, people who had gone through their initiation decades before. Grandmother also had wisdom. Wolf. Altai approached the bridge, bowing one last time to Batuldzii, the only one present with the gift of song. Woman. She bowed to shaman Munkhjargal who bore the gift of foresight, something Sarangerel suspected was quite rare. Wolf. Altai loped across the ribbon of starlight, her form blending into the brightness. When she could no longer be seen, the Celestial Wolf recalled its bridge.

Batuldzii's voice carried out over the steppes, praising the Great Altai Wolf. The tune seemed familiar, though Sarangerel was certain she'd never heard it before. She closed her eyes and let herself be carried by the music, up into the mountains and out across the land. She was disappointed when he reached the end. Her trembling had subsided, and she was suddenly very tired. From the position of the moon, far more time had passed than she'd expected.

Grandmother's warm arm slipped around her shoulders. "We'll head home, now."

"Are we running late?" Sarangerel asked. It would be morning before they returned, and she didn't remember past initiations going so late.

A mischievous smile grew on the old woman's face. "It will take less time to return."

That didn't make sense. On the way out they were fresh and could keep a steady pace. Now, it was the middle of the night and they'd been up for hours.

"Look inside and you will find it," Grandmother said,

patting Sarangerel's shoulder. Then she stepped back. She bent forward turning into a silvery wolf before her hands touched the ground. Flashing a canine grin, she turned and bounded off to join others who'd changed form.

The presence of wolves would have terrified her only hours earlier, and before her initiation she would not have believed what she saw. Closing her eyes, Sarangerel tried to remember what she'd felt during the initiation in an effort to identify what was different now. She was certain the cold had been magic. The snapping sensation in her chest was more than she'd originally assumed. Not only had she been made whole, something had been unlocked; potential had been made real. Altai herself effortlessly went from wolf to woman from moment to moment. Maybe there was no trick.

Sarangerel decided she wanted to be a wolf, and she was. The change was too easy. If they wanted to keep this ability a secret from the rest of the world, it clearly had to be locked away until one could control the impulse. No wonder initiation occurred once childhood had been left behind. She loped over to Temurvachir and Delgernandjil, finding the movement both new yet natural. Her friends stared around in wonder and confusion. Sarangerel knew that thinking strongly of being herself wouldn't change her back, because the wolf was as much herself as the human shape. Instead, she willed herself to be a woman again.

Delgernandjil gaped at her. Given the circumstances, Sarangerel excused the rudeness of such blatant emotions.

"How did you do that?" Temurvachir asked, his expression eager.

"Grandmother told me to look inside," Sarangerel said, touching the center of her chest with three fingers. "It's much simpler than that. You're a wolf, Temurvachir. As we all are by our lineage."

"But how do we change?" he asked, a hint of desperation in his voice.

"It's not really a change," Sarangerel said, realizing that was the wrong word to be using. "It's just another way we can look. Like smiling or speaking, all you have to do, is do it."

Delgernandjil dropped to all fours in an instant, letting out a yelp of surprise that made Sarangerel giggle. Casting her friend a disdainful look, Delgernandjil nudged Temurvachir's thigh with her nose.

That was enough, and he assumed his wolf shape. Then the three of them joined the rest of their clan collecting small bundles from the pile to carry in their teeth on the way home.

* * *

Sarangerel was dipping her bucket into the water when she smelled Galchinua. Like switching to her wolf form, her enhanced sense of smell was easy to adjust to. It felt natural. She waited until the sound of his feet treading over small rocks stopped, then she straightened up, but didn't turn. It had been three days since her initiation, and she'd barely seen him. She'd hoped to talk to him last night when Grandmother invited him to dinner, but he'd had watch and couldn't stay.

"It's no fun to sneak up on you if you let me," he said quietly.

She looked over her shoulder at him. "Are you certain I knew you were there?"

He nodded. Displaying uncharacteristic shyness, he looked down as he took her buckets. "Why did you let me?"

She shrugged. "I was curious what you would do if you succeeded." It was strange to feel awkward around him. The sound of his voice was still enough to make her pulse race, so she was sure all was not lost.

He looked puzzled. "I've never expected to."

"Come," she said, taking his hand lightly in her own and drawing him toward their large flat rock baking in the sun by the river.

He sat beside her, tense and nervous. "Something about you is different."

"Yes." There was no point denying it, even if she couldn't explain. "But I'm still me. I'm still the same person I was before my initiation."

He glanced at her, his face full of doubt. "Have you changed your mind?" he asked. "About our plans, I mean."

106

She shook her head. "No." She wouldn't talk him into anything he didn't want, but she could see now how he could benefit from his own initiation. His presence would become something more. A gift of leadership on top of that would make him amazing no matter where he went. He could excel in a business or a factory, or even here among the people. She also understood that there would be great advantage if the two of them left. They could gain skills and knowledge to help lead their people in a modern world that couldn't be wholly avoided. They would have Altai's blessing wherever they went. She didn't require this isolated transhumant life; that was a choice. Their children could come to Altai in their turn, no matter where they lived.

"Are you sure?" he asked.

"Have you changed your mind?" she asked, fearing his questions had less to do with her feelings than his. "Are you still courting me?"

"Am I still courting you?" he demanded. "I would cross a desert of fire for you."

She closed her eyes and sighed with relief. "Good," she whispered.

"Good?" he asked, confused.

She looked at him again and nodded. "The things you're asking... I thought maybe you didn't want me anymore."

He let out a snort as if to say she was being ridiculous. "Of course I want you." His hesitation was back. "I'm just not sure..." he took her hand and traced a finger lightly over the lines of her palm. "I'm not sure I deserve you."

"What do you mean?" How could he think such a thing?

It took a long time for him to answer. "It's strange. I've never felt this way. You're different. You're still my Moonbeam, and I still love you. But you suddenly seem out of reach."

She shook her head, wrapping both her hands around his. "I'm not." She assured him. She'd had a similar feeling when she first realized he was courting her.

He lifted her hands to his lips, kissing each of them on the back. "I think I see now what I need to do." He raised his head to meet her eyes. "I'm going to do the initiation."

"Are you sure?" she asked, hoping he couldn't see how she felt about that.

He nodded. "My earlier decision may have been misinformed."

"I hope you're doing it because you want to, not because of me," she said firmly.

He gave her crooked smile. "What if it's both?"

"Both?"

"I want to do it," he said. "Seeing how it's changed you is a part of that." This had been what the others meant when they said she would convince him. "Though, I still have to wait until the next full moon," he said.

"And your birthday," she added.

His face lit with a mischievous smile. "Yes. That comes sooner. Then I'll be able to court you in earnest."

"I thought you were already doing that," she said, happiness filling her heart.

He shook his head. "That's just been practice. After all, I'm much too young to be seeking your hand."

"At the moment." It was hard to hold in the giggles.

"And for a few more days," he agreed. He gently touched the tip of her nose. "But I have big plans to win you over once I'm seventeen."

"You aren't going to have to work that hard." She grinned.

"No spoiling my plans," he said, pretending to be stern. "If I'm going to win you over, I have to do it right." He leaned closer and whispered in her ear. "And I fully intend to do so." He kissed her hands one last time before standing up.

"You're going?" She followed him off the rock.

"I have things to do," he told her. He picked up her staff and held it out to her. "I need to talk to my parents and the Shaman if I'm going to be ready in time."

Lightfoot

Lory had been hunting for hours when he realized that he didn't recognize his surroundings. At first he wasn't concerned. He'd hunted more times than he could count this year alone. He'd been drilled in survival techniques since he was old enough to walk; surely he could find his way home.

The village was just northeast of the great forest, so Lory started walking that direction. Once he reached the edge of the forest, it would be a snap to get home. Although it was always dim within the forest, light filtered down through the trees, dappling the brown and green ground with bright yellow splotches. Certain he'd find his way right before dark, he set off in a cheerful mood.

After walking for some time, Lory stopped to reassess his situation. He looked around and saw a small pine tree that looked strangely familiar. He rubbed his eyes and took a few breaths to clear his mind. He hadn't felt this disoriented in the woods since his first hunting trip years ago. He'd been walking the right way, hadn't he? The sun's position was concealed by the treetops and, contrary to belief, moss grew wherever it wanted in the forest.

Stories came to mind of well-seasoned villagers who'd disappeared. All sorts of disasters had been known to befall travelers in general, especially those who traversed the forest. Lory had always been certain such tales were designed to frighten children and make the usual hunt seem much more dangerous than it really was. His father insisted that those who perished had panicked. Lory shook his head and pushed down the fear he was beginning to feel. The only way to survive in the forest was to keep his head. He'd be fine.

His rumbling stomach stopped him next, reminding him that he hadn't eaten since sun-up. He reached into his leather shoulder bag for the pemmican he always took hunting. He looked around more intently while he gnawed on the bar of dried grains, nuts and fruit. Perhaps he'd missed a known tree or path. After walking for so long, he should be close to familiar surroundings. But all the trees looked the same. The only tracks on the pine needle-littered forest floor were human-made scuffs, but they were fresh. He bent to examine them, noticing as he did, that they also went to the northeast. Whoever left the tracks dragged their heels as if they were tired. He shrugged and stood up, heartened by this discovery. If others had been this direction recently, he must be going the right way.

He turned and looked directly at a disturbingly familiar small pine tree. A wave of nausea washed over him and he forced himself to breathe slowly. He was not some foolish inexperienced child, and he refused to believe that he'd been walking in circles. There were lots of small pine trees in the forest. Big trees had to grow up from somewhere, after all. But few of them were perfectly symmetrical. Determined to get a grip on his fear, he reached for the small ball of blue yarn he kept in his pocket. He tied a short piece of yarn to the lead of the tree, then smiled, satisfied. The part of his mind in a panic would be reassured the next time he saw a small pine tree, because it wouldn't be marked with blue yarn.

He started on his way again, finally admitting that he was lost. He should have been able to recognize something, but he couldn't. Where had he gotten himself? He'd wandered in the forest any number of times, and he'd always come home. Why should this time be any different? He reminded himself that other hunters had died because they'd made a mistake; one was all it took. He sighed wearily and mused over the time. The forest was darker than it had been earlier, and he guessed it must be near evening. His father and brothers would be looking for him by now. Would they be worried? He dragged his heels as he focused on the pine needle muddled footprints in front of him. It looked like there was more than one set, and he wondered if they had been left by his father and brothers.

He'd been trudging along in a half-daze when the eerie howl of a single wolf startled him. Lory stiffened and looked around. Wolves were the most unpredictable of all creatures, and that one hadn't been far off. He reminded himself that a single wolf wasn't a threat and that the howl could have just sounded close because it carried through the still air. He began to relax, until he focused on a small tree. A short length of blue yarn waved from the lead of the perfectly symmetrical pine.

Numb and confused, he stumbled to the little tree. He recognized the knot as his own, and he sank to his knees in despair. How could this be? As hard as it was to accept, he'd been walking in circles all day. The wolf howled again, this time answered by another. Lory whimpered in fear as he cowered close to the little tree. He'd been stupid not to pay attention to where he was walking in the first place. He grabbed for the lead branch, hardly noticing the prick of the needles, as if touching it would make it all go away. His mind was certainly too addled to find his way out of the maze of trees. He was exhausted, but even fresh he couldn't hope to outrun wolves. He'd gotten lost, through no fault but his own, and now he was going to die. He wondered how long it would take the wolves to kill him. His gun would be of no use. He'd heard about wolf attacks as a child; he wouldn't be able to reload fast enough, he'd run out of bullets, and they would keep coming. They would tear him apart. He shivered, still clinging to the forgotten little tree.

A twig snapped behind him, and he spun to face the danger. He froze and blinked in confusion. These were no wolves. A girl held tightly to the hand of a young woman. They stood in a patch of light and the sun reflected off their hair like twin halos, making them seem not entirely of this earth. They had nearly black hair, and their high cheekbones gave their faces an exotic cast. Unlike village women, who favored wool or cotton dresses with bright designs, they wore close fitting leather trews and durable homespun tunics. Each wore a dark vest with only the stitching and cut for design. They looked at home among the trees. Lory stared at them as he tried to get his mind to comprehend what was happening.

"Have you lost your way?" the woman asked in a quiet voice.

Lory nodded. She seemed so calm and self-assured he couldn't help but blurt out, "I've been walking circles all day, and now the wolves are coming!"

She smiled, trying not to laugh. "They won't hurt you."

He stared at her, wondering for a moment if she was a tree spirit. Although they'd come out of nowhere with hardly any warning, she looked human, not at all what he would have expected of a sprite.

"They're just curious who you are, and what you're doing in their territory," she said in a reassuring voice.

"How do you know?" he demanded, not ready to be convinced.

"My family has lived in this forest for centuries," she said proudly. She took a step closer to him. "Come. It's too late this day to put your path to rights, and we wouldn't want to exhibit poor hospitality to a stranger lost in our midst." Although wary, she seemed amused.

Lory clambered to his feet, feeling clumsy and foolish in front of this woman who was so much more confident than he.

"Is he one of our people?" the girl whispered, glancing up at the young woman before looking at Lory again.

The older one shook her head. "Certainly not. He is simply a man who has found his way here, but can not find his way back." The look she gave the girl was enough to prevent further questioning. She turned back to Lory. "And what is your name, stranger, that we may address you more appropriately?"

"I'm Lory Jalonack," he said, finally taking a step closer to them. "I'm from a village just northeast of the forest."

"I thought as much," she said with a nod. "It's too far to go tonight, and you must surely be tired."

The relief of being rescued made him light-headed. Lory numbly took the hand she offered him, and followed where she led.

After a minute or two he was calm enough to be curious about her and he watched her as they walked. Her bangs were pulled back in a thin braid, and she wore the rest of her hair loose, hanging to her waist. Her eyes were a brown so light they almost appeared to be amber. She was several inches shorter than him, but then, he was tall. Her feet hardly made a sound as she walked through the detritus littering the forest floor. Her sister was equally silent, and he felt like a big oaf clomping noisily through the underbrush next to them.

Ignoring his intent appraisal, the young woman introduced herself. "I'm Kiana, and this is my sister Kenzie." She smiled down at the girl.

"I've been learning my way about the forest," Kenzie said with a smile.

"That's a good idea," Lory said, looking at the girl. She was nearly a miniature of her sister, down to the amber colored eyes. She wore her hair in a tight braid that swung midway down her back. "Especially if you're to live here all your life." It was one thing to visit the forest for a day of hunting, but his people avoided extended stays or travels through the forest. He'd never heard of folk settling here. It was a dark place full of equally dark creatures, although this was truly the first time he'd ever been afraid. "You wouldn't want to get lost."

"Like you did?" Kenzie asked with a grin.

"Kenzie, let's show Mr. Jalonack how polite we can be, shall we?" Kiana said in mild rebuke.

Kenzie looked down, feigning hurt feelings.

"Oh, that's all right," Lory said quickly. "I did get lost, and I guess I deserve a bit of ribbing." He managed a shy smile for

Kiana, who looked up at him. "Please call me Lory."

Kiana smiled and nodded, then turned back to her sister again. "Now, Kenzie, let's see how well you paid attention," she said, her voice matter-of-fact. "How do we get home?"

Kenzie looked up, eager for the challenge. She released her sister's hand and very deliberately began to lead the way through the forest.

The girl ran a hand over the bark of a tree in passing, before turning in a different direction. From the smile on Kiana's face, Lory thought little Kenzie must be guiding them correct. The girl paused briefly and sniffed at the air. She looked to one side and the other. He held his breath, as if the slightest sound might distract her. Kiana squeezed his hand, and he looked down at her in surprise.

She smiled reassuringly up at him. "Don't be troubled. I know the whole forest. And Kenzie knows enough to get us home from here."

Part of his mind insisted it was impossible for her to know the entire forest, but her confidence implied honesty. "Then she knows more than me," he admitted ruefully. Kiana was very pretty, and he was pleased she hadn't let go of his hand. He cautioned himself not to jump to conclusions; she was probably just a good person who was kind to strangers. He knew nothing of these forest folk, and at her age she could already be promised to someone. Besides, she likely thought him an idiot for getting lost in the forest she called home. Kiana pulled on his hand, and he realized that Kenzie had started off again.

Kenzie paused abruptly and pointed down into the ravine that ran beside them. "Oh, look Kee!"

Kiana pulled Lory after and turned to see what had pleased her sibling. She smiled. "Aren't they magnificent?" she asked.

Kenzie nodded, speechless.

Lory stared in horror as a pack of wolves, probably seven in all, raced through the ravine below. Oblivious to the humans, the wolves maintained their course. The drumming of their feet was reminiscent of several horses at a gallop, as they sped over the uneven ground, neither slowing nor stopping to navigate the hazards. He felt frozen, unable to back away or run. He watched as first one, then another disappeared in the dark woods. He held his breath until the last one had passed from his sight.

"Don't squeeze so hard Lory," Kiana said quietly. "You'll break my hand."

To his surprise, he'd tightened his grip on her hand without even realizing it. He looked down, embarrassed and released her hand. Kiana, however, didn't let go of his.

"Are you afraid of wolves?" Kenzie asked, looking at him in confusion.

Lory nodded, feeling a coward in the presence of this child who clearly had no such fear.

"But why?" she demanded in bewilderment.

"Kenzie," Kiana interrupted. "Supper will be served without us if we don't move on."

The girl took the hint, but gave her sister a brief frown. Her expression indicated that she wanted to know how she was to learn anything if she wasn't allowed to question the stranger.

"What's your village like?" Kiana asked, glancing at him out of the corner of her eye.

"It's much like any other village, I imagine," he said quietly, still ashamed.

"Have you been to other villages?" Kenzie asked, peeking over her shoulder at the stranger, but avoiding her sister's eyes.

"Oh yes." He nodded. "Some are a little bigger, and others are a little smaller."

"But what does it look like?" Kenzie asked plaintively. "I've never been to a village before."

"You haven't?" he asked in surprise. Surely these folks must trade with nearby villages.

"I'm too little to go with," she said in disgust.

"You'll get to go this year, if you behave," Kiana reminded her. "And it's not as if you haven't traveled."

"We've got the usual houses and shops. The communal center is in the middle of town," Lory said as he struggled to create a description of what had always been familiar to him. "Most folks are farmers, but there are a few herdsmen, merchants and other entrepreneurs. There's a lot of open space, and not too many trees." He would have liked a few more trees on those hot days.

"Farmers?" Kenzie asked, carefully enunciating the new word.

"They cultivate great patches of land for specific food plants," Kiana explained in an off-handed manner.

"Big gardens?" Kenzie asked.

Lory smiled, amused by the analogy. "Huge gardens." It hadn't occurred to him that they might not farm, but then, plants needed more sun than they would get here.

"Are you a farmer then, Lory?" Kiana asked.

"My father is, and we all help out, but..." He shrugged. "I'd rather be doing just about anything else. I was hunting today, and prefer that to planting or tilling." He'd been relieved when he found an apprenticeship outside of farming.

"So you wish to be a hunter?" Kiana asked with a gleam in her amber eyes.

"We're very good hunters," Kenzie said proudly.

"You hunt?" he asked in surprise as he looked at the little girl. He'd never met a girl who wanted to hunt, much less knew how. Village girls had no interest in what was commonly viewed as a man's responsibility. Although he couldn't be sure of her age, Kenzie looked younger than he'd been when he got his first arquebus lesson.

"We all hunt," Kiana said with a smile. "It's part of our way of life."

Lory nodded. That would make sense. "I guess you could say that everyone in the village has a special skill, and we trade with each other to get what we need or want."

"What's your skill Lory?" Kenzie asked.

"I build things." He looked at the little girl. "I've been training with an older man in the village, and eventually that will be my trade, the skill I exchange for other things."

"What do you build?" Kiana asked.

"Houses, mostly," he said, trying to catch her eye. He would be guaranteed a secure financial future in nearly any village, and he wanted her to know that. Just in case it mattered. "But I also build barns and anything someone wants to pay me for. A lot of the time I just repair older buildings, though," he confessed. New buildings weren't needed as often as repairs were, and that paid well enough.

"You're good at making repairs to old buildings?" Kiana asked suddenly.

He nodded, startled by her eagerness.

"Oh, that's wonderful," Kiana said with a smile. "I mean " she looked down, appearing flustered for the first time.

"Have you something that needs repairs?" he asked gently, although inside he was thrilled. He felt he owed her something, besides, he would gladly take any opportunity to get to know her better.

"Have we ever!" Kenzie said with a laugh.

Kiana looked appalled by her sister's forward response.

Feeling an advantage for the first time since they found him, he dared to give Kiana's hand a gentle squeeze. When she looked up at him, he smiled. "I've been a right fool, getting myself lost, and I don't know what I'd have done if you hadn't found me. At least let me make it up to you by doing what I can."

Kiana smiled shyly and nodded. "You may regret that offer."

He briefly wondered if her earlier moment of hesitation and embarrassment were an act to draw him in. "We'll see about that." They reached the top of a small hill, and Lory could see a sturdy stone house at the bottom. There were no small trees or bushes in the area just surrounding the house, giving the feeling of a yard. The large old-growth trees had been left, keeping the house in the shadow of the forest's canopy. Lory saw a garden off to one side and an impressive half-timber barn behind the house.

"I did it!" Kenzie shouted as she jumped about with glee. "I got us home!"

Kiana shook her head and smiled. "As if you didn't think you could."

"I found my way home!" Kenzie ran down the hill shouting for the attention of others. "We're home! We've brought back a stranger!"

Kiana dropped Lory's hand and gestured for him to accompany her down to the house. He regretted the absence of her comforting fingers around his own, but he reminded himself that he didn't know anything about these people. Kenzie had spread the news, and by the time he reached the bottom of the hill with Kiana, they were met by a crowd of others. As they circled around, Lory was surprised to realize that so many people lived in the forest. He wondered if some of them were merely visiting. Was it even possible that they were all one family?

"Lory," Kiana said from his side. "I welcome you to the homestead of the Lightfoots." She turned to an older looking couple. "This is Lory Jalonack."

The man looked at Lory for a moment, as if measuring him up. He grunted. "Got lost, did you?"

Lory nodded, uncomfortable under the man's scrutiny. "Kiana and Kenzie found me before the wolves could."

That elicited a bark of laughter from the man. "They found you before the wolves, huh?" He shot Kiana a grin. "Well, it was good of them to bring you back for the night."

"Father," Kiana said politely.

Lory couldn't see how this man could be her father. Other than the amber eyes, she bore no resemblance to him. His gray-shot black hair was almost shaggy, more reminiscent of fur than hair. He was a big man, tall and stocky, while Kiana and Kenzie were more delicate. Both looked more like the woman standing next to her father, and Lory decided she must be their mother. Were these all her children, he wondered. There seemed too many.

"Father, he repairs buildings," she said quickly.

He turned back to Lory, his manner considerably improved. "Do you now?"

Before Lory could respond, Kiana had. "He said he'd look at ours, though I think it may be more work than he expected."

"Well, it'd be a blessing nonetheless." He offered Lory a hand. "Lucas Lightfoot, head of the Lightfoot pack."

Lory shook the man's hand.

"You'll stay on for a few days, then? You'll not lack for the necessities, and we'll help you as we can. Although it'd be best if you'd try to blend in a bit." Lucas gave Lory one last scrutinizing stare then pointed to the arquebus still slung over his shoulder. "And under no circumstance is that thing to come in the house," he said firmly, almost sounding angry.

"I'll unload it," Lory offered willingly, surprised by the man's vehemence.

"No guns."

"Yes sir." His quick compliance won him a pleased smile from Lucas.

Lory extracted the bullet before hanging his gun in the narrow shed outside the front door. There were too many kids about to leave a loaded gun around. Kiana watched as he slipped the bullet into a small leather sack which went into his shoulder bag. He would have to ask her later how they hunted. He was also curious why her father seemed so resentful toward guns.

After the immediate excitement, everyone returned to their interrupted duties. Aware that they were being watched from nearly every angle, despite her family's apparent diligence to their tasks, he followed Kiana to wash up before dinner. The pump wasn't far from the garden, and the water was cold.

"So why does your father call your family a pack?" he asked as he toweled his face and hands dry.

Kiana smiled secretively. "My people are not like yours, Lory."

He snorted. "I'd guessed that much." People who embraced the wilderness the way her family had would likely be very different from those who feared it. After generations of such a life, he wondered what disparities had developed.

She thought a moment, then gestured for him to follow her to a downed tree. "I suppose it's only fair to prepare you a little. While you're with us you're going to hear and see a lot of things that may seem very odd to you." She settled herself on the log and waited for him to sit beside her. "Remember how Kenzie reacted when you said you were afraid of wolves?"

He nodded. It was one of many things he wished he could forget.

"My whole family would have that same reaction, although

the older ones have learned to expect it from your people." She glanced across the yard to the barn. "We see the wolf as... well, she's our sister. We've learned a great deal from wolves. Indeed we never would have survived here without the knowledge they've given us."

Lory tried not to stare at her, lest it should project his horror. He'd been raised with a different ideology and had difficulty seeing that there could be any good in the animals his people damned as purely evil.

"They're very social animals, living in family groups, just like we do," she explained. "To my people, it's desirable to emulate the wolf."

"And that's why you refer to your family as a pack?" he asked, trying to accept it calmly. That a group of people would worship the wolf's way of life almost seemed blasphemous.

Kiana nodded. "But that's not all," she cautioned. "Like wolves, we have a very well established hierarchy, and no one would act out of line according to his or her place in the pack."

He never would have imagined that wolves lived in such a structured social setting. "What is your place?" he asked. She seemed to have a great many brothers and sisters, and she'd implied that there were a limited number of positions of rank.

She smiled and straightened up with a measure of dignity. "I am beta female."

"What's beta?" he stumbled over the unfamiliar term.

With a little laugh she got to her feet. "Alpha is the highest."

"That would be Lucas, your father," Lory said quickly. He'd seen the way everyone deferred to him.

Kiana nodded. "He's the alpha male, but there is always a female counterpart."

Lory got to his feet and followed her as she walked toward the house.

"Kota is Lucas' counterpart, and together they lead the pack. They're pretty well established as alphas, and no one is bold enough to challenge their authority," she explained, emphasizing the last word. "Among the rest of us, rank is often swapped about.

Seniority has little to do with it, so it's not always oldest who has the highest rank."

He turned to her, baffled by the custom. "Do you realize how confusing that is?" Lory asked. How was he to keep straight who was superior to whom if they continually challenged each other for position? The last thing he wanted to do was offend his hosts.

"It's really not that hard once you get used to it," she assured him. "You can usually gauge rank on interactions." She pointed to a group of children.

Lory recognized Kenzie with the other kids, and smiled when he saw how they idolized her.

"We call her little alpha," Kiana said with considerable pride. "They're too young yet to earn an adult rank, and kids get away with a lot, just like puppies."

"But they follow the same rules," he said as he began to recognize an order to the children's conduct.

"See, I told you it wasn't too tough." Kiana smiled. "In their group Kenzie is alpha, and she's too strong-minded to be bumped down. The rest have to fight each other for the other titles."

Lory shook his head. "I'm sorry Kiana, but it's all so strange."

She nodded. "Maybe it won't seem so after a while. If you're open-minded. Many of your people are too stuck in their beliefs to permit us ours."

"You may have to explain things to me, and I'll try to understand," he assured her quickly. Her good opinion meant much to him, and he didn't want to be like the others she'd mentioned with distaste. "But it'll take some getting used to," he admitted.

She shrugged but smiled up at him. "Supper is ready, and you must be hungry after a day in the woods."

"I'm starved," he said. He followed Kiana around to the front door of the big house. For all its apparent age, it had been designed and built very well. "You know," he said, as he paused in the doorway. "This house is incredible."

Kiana glanced at him over her shoulder. "What do you mean?"

"Well... it'll easily stand for another hundred years." He examined the walls of the entryway with professional interest. "This kind of craftsmanship is almost lost to my people. Few take the time to build something that will last like this anymore."

Kiana smiled. "It has stood the test of time," she said, quite pleased with his praise. "Lightfoots have lived in this house for over five centuries." She let out a little laugh when Lory turned to her in surprise. "Although we've lived in the area for longer still."

"This house is over five hundred years old?" He'd never seen anything that old. He turned back to the wall he'd just looked at. "My village isn't even two hundred." His mind reeled with the staggering fact that her family had lived in the forest long before areas had been cleared out for the villages he'd grown up with. It would have been an even larger and more dangerous place back then.

Kiana grinned, looking quite pleased. "My people were meant to live here, Lory. It will ever be our home."

Still awestruck, Lory followed her into a large common room. The family was settling at a long table that occupied most of the space. There was a smaller table off to one side, and the younger children were gathering there. Kiana pulled him to an empty spot big enough for them both and introduced him to her brother Fang, who sat on Lory's other side.

"Fang, this is Lory. He's going to help us with some repairs tomorrow," she said as she handed plates down their side of the table.

Fang gave Lory a penetrating stare. "Got lost, didja?"

"Fang," her voice snapped in sharp reprimand.

He looked away, chastised.

Fang was near his own age, Lory thought, perhaps a little younger. He clearly fell below Kiana in the hierarchy she'd mentioned earlier.

The Lightfoots evidently didn't set the table before sitting down. Kiana and the young man across the table from her, began passing down plates and silverware. Lory passed to Fang, who kept his head down and avoided making eye contact. He wondered if that sort of display was part of observing his position.

Lucas and Kota came through a door at the end of the room, and from their burdens, Lory guessed it was the kitchen. Although there had been a great deal of talking and noise beforehand, the room suddenly went silent. Another of Kiana's siblings, by the look of him, followed with a platter bearing the carcass of a wild pig.

"Mouka gets the honor of the table tonight," Kiana whispered to Lory. "It was his success that will feed us."

Lory nodded. This boy had killed the boar then, and had earned some sort of recognition.

Mouka stood at the head of the table, between Lucas and Kota. Once he was sure he had everyone's attention, he held up his left hand. "Hail swiftness and stealth of mien," he said in a firm but sober tone.

"Hail swiftness and stealth of mien," the family responded in solemn unison.

Lory looked around in uneasy fascination. Perhaps this was what Kiana had meant about witnessing unusual things tonight. He'd never heard a prayer of this sort, but Mouka's words had a distinctly invocatory quality to them.

"Glory to the worthy beast," Mouka's hand hesitated, palm up, over the carcass.

"Glory to the worthy beast," the family repeated.

"For one to live, one must die," he flipped his hand over and touched the back of the boar with the tips of his fingers.

"For one to live, one must die."

"For strength of will and sight and mind, we praise the light of foot," Mouka finished with a proud smile.

"For strength of will and sight and mind, we praise the light of foot." Promptly after this response, Kota started a simple rhythm by thumping on the table with her fists. The whole family joined in, slapping and banging the table in front of them. Lucas and Kota began to chant the boy's name. "Mou-ka, Mou-ka, Mou-ka."

Kiana and Fang picked up the chant, and Lory looked

around the room. Although part of him was uneasy enough to want to leave, he found the ritual too provocative to disregard. Mouka looked pleased and embarrassed at the same time. Even the little children were chanting in time with their pounding fists. From this exhibition alone, Lory had the feeling that this family was bound much tighter than his own.

With an abruptness that left him unsettled, the ceremony was over and supper was being served. Lory looked at Kiana, hoping to ask her a few questions about what he'd just seen, but she was occupied with the platters Lucas was handing to her. The rest of the family carried on as before, talking, teasing, and joking, as if nothing special had happened. Lory was nudged from the right and he turned to look at Fang.

"Do you honor the one who hunts for your table?" he asked in a low voice, almost as if afraid to be overheard.

Lory shrugged. "Not really. It's just expected."

Fang looked at him in disbelief. "It's expected here too, but..." He shook his head. "There will always be the hungry times, when prey is elusive Even the best hunters fail to bring home meat," he insisted. "The one who feeds us deserves reverence because it is their skill and effort that lets us live to see another day."

Lory thought for a moment. "For one to live, one must die?" he asked, quoting Mouka's reverent words.

Fang nodded solemnly. "There are times when it is the prey who lives."

Lory stared at him in awful understanding. He expected life in the forest to be a challenge, but he hadn't thought it would be such a basic fight for survival.

"Here Lory," Kiana said, calling back his attention. She handed him a bowl of white roots, sliced thinly and steamed.

He took the bowl and gave himself a small serving.

"You needn't starve yourself," she said as she directed Fang to put the bowl down. "There's more than enough."

"But food is harder to find in the forest, I don't want to short you any," he insisted. He couldn't bear the thought of her starving. Or little Kenzie.

Kiana patted his hand but served him more roots. "This isn't the hungry season, and there's plenty. It's a credit to you that you are thoughtful, but tonight we feast."

"What about tomorrow?"

She smiled. "We are always aware of the dangers in our way of life, Lory. That's why we honor the one whose hunt is successful. It reminds us, daily, that we're only here for a short time, and that we're much smaller than we like to think we are." She passed him a bowl of raw greens. "Now eat."

Still feeling uncomfortable, he joined the feasting. It wasn't until he'd eaten several bites that he realized how hungry was. All he'd had to sustain himself since breakfast was a bit of pemmican, and there was no knowing how many miles he'd actually walked.

He looked up now and again to see what was happening around him, but the rest of the meal was not so different from his own family's customs. Some people talked as they ate, while others bent to their plates with purpose. Mouka was seated at the head of the table, between Kota and Lucas. It was clearly a place of honor, and Lory wondered what they did if more than one individual had a successful hunt on a given day. He turned to Fang, who was snatching covert glances at the guest as often as he dared.

"Have you received honor of the table?" Lory quietly asked.

Fang nearly choked as he started to laugh. "I wouldn't be sitting here if I hadn't," he said proudly. At Lory's blank look, he continued. "Until you earn honor of the table, you sit over there," he turned his thumb toward the smaller table crowded with children.

Lory nodded. It was a graduation of sorts from the children's rank to an adult.

Fang tapped the table in front of himself. "I may be omega, but I'm first rank omega. And I wouldn't sit here if I didn't deserve it."

"So the seating arrangement is based on rank?" Lory asked, ignoring the unfamiliar terms for the moment.

Fang nodded.

Lory looked back to the head of the table. Mouka sat at the very end, flanked by his parents. Kiana sat next to her father, making her just beneath him on the ladder. "Kiana said she's beta female," he whispered to Fang. "Is beta directly after alpha?"

Fang nodded. "Kee is very strong. I don't think many of our sisters would even think of challenging her. Kenzie might when she's older, but Kee'll likely be gone by then."

"But where would she go?" Lory asked in alarm. Surely she wasn't expected to die before Kenzie grew up. She seemed too proud of her family and it's history in the forest to simply leave.

Fang gave Lory and odd look. "We aren't the only pack in the forest, you know."

"You're not?" He remembered then that Kiana had mentioned traveling.

Fang shook his head. "Of course not."

"She would leave to join another pack?" he asked.

Fang shrugged. "She could even start her own new pack. The forest is big enough and abundant enough for several other packs." A dark look crossed his face and he turned away.

Despite Lory's interest in the conversation, Fang wouldn't look at him for the rest of the meal. Kiana was busy talking to her father, and Lory regretted having monopolized so much of her time. As second in charge, she must surely have duties that his presence had kept her from. He sat quietly until Kenzie appeared at his side.

"Come play with us Lory," she begged as she reached for his hand.

No one else had left the table, and he wasn't certain of proper protocol. "I'm not sure I should, Kenzie. Others are still eating."

"They won't mind," she insisted as she wrinkled up her face.

Fang finally looked up and nodded. "Kids get away with almost anything they want. And if she wants you to play, you can go."

Lory quietly got up. There was a distinct lull in conversation as he followed the girl to the door. He glanced back to the table once and saw Kiana smiling, so he continued on his way certain that Kenzie and Fang hadn't led him wrong.

The rest of the children were waiting outside when Kenzie and Lory joined them. During dinner the sky had darkened further, and Lory squinted as he looked around the yard. Lamplight would have helped, but any fire in the forest would have to be closely monitored to prevent disaster.

"Let's play chase," Kenzie suggested. The other children eagerly agreed, bouncing and squealing as they expressed their interest.

"What's chase?" Lory asked perplexed. As it turned out, chase was exactly as it sounded. One person had to chase the lot of them until they tired of the game. As the adult, he was declared the chaser and the children quickly spread about the yard. The children were faster than he'd expected, and it took a while before he caught even one of them. More accustomed to the lighting and the area, the children were often able to slip past him.

Exhausted, and way past his second wind, Lory determined the only way to end the game was to catch the instigator. Kenzie had successfully evaded capture each time he'd tried. He turned until he found her, standing in the shadow of a tree. He crouched slightly as he focused on her. It was too dark to know for certain, but he thought he could see her grinning at him.

"You can't catch me, Lory," she teased. "I'm too fast."

"Speed isn't everything, Kenzie." He took one slow step toward her, then another.

"It's just the most important thing," she responded calmly.

He needed to be ready and he needed to be quick. Speed was important, but cunning was even more so. Kenzie broke into a run, and the chase was on. Part of the ritual of the chase was to tease the chaser by running in circles and making abrupt directional changes. Kenzie darted one way, then the other, momentarily cutting within arm's distance before dodging away.

Now that he was concentrating, he could almost feel the moments when she changed direction. There was no pattern, no reason. Kenzie probably didn't even know which direction she was going to go until she did it, which kept her from telegraphing the moves. The next time he felt her start to turn, he turned with her. He dove for her, snatching her in his arms as he tumbled to a stop. Lory was never sure who was more surprised by his success, Kenzie or himself.

"You okay?" he asked as he brushed the dirt off her knees.

"How'd you do that?" she demanded, indignant. "You aren't supposed to be able to catch me. You're not even like us."

"I told you speed wasn't everything." He'd a few years of hunting on her yet, but she'd learn to feel the prey eventually. He chuckled as he got to his feet, hauling the girl up over his shoulder as he did. She squealed, first in fear, then in delight. "So's the game over then?"

"Put me down and I'll tell you," she offered.

"You're more likely to run off again if I do that, now, aren't you?" He spun in a circle and felt her giggling before he heard it.

"Do that again!"

"What?" he asked, playing dumb. He turned in a circle the other way. "Oh, that?" he asked when she laughed again.

"Again, Lory, again!"

"What? And make you sick?" He spun her one last time before they reached the house. When he looked up, he realized that Kiana was standing by the door watching him, and there were faces peering out the windows. He crouched down and gently set Kenzie back on her feet. He straightened up and looked at Kiana, wondering if he'd done something wrong.

"You caught her?" Kiana asked quietly.

Lory nodded and smiled. "Can't say I'd be able to do it again, though."

Kiana grinned. "I wouldn't have guessed you could do it once." She turned to Kenzie. "Bed time."

Kenzie made a face.

"I mean it," Kiana said firmly. "And that goes for the rest of you pups," she called out into the yard.

The children filed quietly into the house under their sister's watchful eye.

"Are they always this obedient?" Lory asked in surprise. He'd never known a child to so willingly go to bed.

"Oh goodness, no," she said with a hint of a laugh. "They're not so different from your village children as that. But they do know when to behave."

Lory followed Kiana back into the large common room. Those who'd been looking out the windows had gone back to their routines. Fang was playing a game with one of his brothers, and Lucas was reclining in a chair, his feet up on a small bench. Kota was no where to be seen, and Lory wondered if she was preparing the children for bed.

"Lucas wants to talk to you," Kiana said, gesturing to the vacancy beside her father.

Lory felt unaccountably nervous as he approached the patriarch of this unusual family. He could almost feel every set of eyes watching him as he paused by Lucas' chair. "You wanted to see me sir?" He was reluctant to sit until he'd been invited to do so.

Lucas looked up and nodded. "Have a seat, Lory. And I won't bite, if that's what's troubling you." His beard nearly hid his smile. Lory sat and waited in uncomfortable silence.
"I thought I'd get to know the young man my daughter brought home. Especially if you're staying with us for a spell."

Lory nodded. "Of course. Is there anything specific you wanted...?"

"How old are you?" Lucas leaped on the opportunity. "I've never been any good at guessing age."

Lory doubted that very much. Lucas seemed too keen to miss a thing. But it was his house, and Lory saw no harm in playing along. "I'm nineteen."

Lucas nodded. "You married? Got any kids?"

Lory shook his head. "No sir."

Lucas stared at him a moment. "No, you're not married? Or no, you haven't any children?"

"Both," Lory said quietly. He'd suspected Lucas was motivated by more than idle curiosity. After all, Lory was still a stranger and the Lightfoots had several daughters whose safety would be of concern.

"Live alone?"

Lory shook his head. "I live with my parents right now. There's really been no need for me to build my own place yet, and they're happy to have me." His parents had even discouraged him from moving out. It helped to have an extra able body on the farm, even if it was only part of the time.

"You come from a big family?"

Lory shook his head again. "Not like yours." Lucas smiled at that comment. "I've two younger brothers and a younger sister."

Lucas nodded. "A family should never be bigger than it can support. Four children is usually on the high end in villages, isn't it?"

Lory shrugged. "There's a few families with six or seven, but they have bigger farms than my father's, or they're merchants."

"Kiana said you'd been hunting when you got lost. Are you a big hunter?"

Lory shrugged again. "Not really. I'm all right, but I usually hunt alone so I don't go after anything I can't carry back out myself."

"So, you hunt anything smaller than what? A fox, a boar, a deer?" Lucas asked, sounding very interested.

For some reason Lory thought Lucas was more concerned with what he *didn't* hunt. "Lots of rabbits," he said. "I get pheasants and occasionally a turkey, but nothing much bigger than that. If I hunted larger animals I'd end up wasting too much."

Lucas nodded. A line of children suddenly appeared in the doorway, and he moved his feet off the bench.

Kenzie led the other children in, pausing beside her father. She climbed up into Lucas's lap, giving him a huge hug once she got there.

"You have a good day, pet?" he asked, smiling as he pulled the child closer.

Kenzie nodded. "I found my way home without even a hint," she said proudly. "And I saw the pack first. And I got to play chase."

"Got caught too," Lucas said.

She nodded, but wasn't so eager to confirm it.

"That doesn't happen often, does it?" Lucas gave her

another hug. "Now you get off to bed so you can do more of the same tomorrow."

"What are we doing tomorrow? Will Lory be here to play with? Do I get to hunt?"

Lucas chuckled at her eagerness. "The dawn will tell, I certainly won't." He lifted her off his lap and started the procedure all over with the next child.

Kenzie took Lory by surprise when she climbed into his lap next. "G'night Lory," she said as she gave him a hug.

Pleased with the unexpected action, he hugged her back. "Pleasant dreams Kenzie."

"Thanks for playing chase with us," she said as she got back to the floor. "It was fun, even if you did catch me."

Kenzie's actions set a precedent, and each child that followed bid first their father, then their guest, good night. When it was Lory's turn to go to bed, he was directed upstairs. He was to bed down with the rest of the Lightfoot males in their room just to the right of the stairs. There was no door, only a curtain, which appeared to be in keeping with the other entrances to rooms on the upper level. The long room was open, with no partitions between the two rows of lumpy bag mattresses. Most of the mattresses were obviously claimed, so Lory found one that looked unused and settled himself in. He'd never spent a night away from home. He'd certainly never stayed at someone else's house before. But he was tired from his long day and quickly fell asleep.

* * *

"Lory, wake up," the voice whispered urgently in his ear. "C'mon, Lory. Wake up."

His shoulder was shaken by two small hands. He opened his eyes and could barely see Kenzie kneeling above him.

"I want to show you something." She grabbed his hand and pulled on him until he sat up. "Come on," she dropped his hand and gestured for him to follow.

She walked toward the window at one end of the long room. "What is it?" he asked in a whisper as he crept behind her. "Is something wrong?"

The girl dropped gently to her hands and knees, hardly

making a sound. "Look," she said as she peered out the window.

Lory lowered himself to look out the window. He could see dark shapes in the yard below. "What..." he backed away from the window in surprise when he realized the shapes were wolves.

Kenzie gave him a disparaging look. "They wouldn't hurt you, even if they came in the house."

Lory swallowed against the lump in his throat and pushed himself back to the window. In the shadowy yard one wolf approached another. It dropped its front end nearly to the ground, its muzzle near its paws, but kept it's wriggling rear and tail in the air. "It's going to attack," Lory said in horror. Kenzie giggled and Lory looked at her in surprise. "What's so funny?"

"That's a play bow, Lory," she said with a grin. "They're playing, not fighting."

He looked back out the window. "Playing?"

"They're hunters by nature, silly. Of course play mimics that."

He shrugged. It made sense, but they looked so vicious. He watched as the two wolves pounced at each other, narrowly missing each others' faces as they snapped their teeth. They stood their ground then, each pushing its open mouth across the other's face. It looked like they were trying to bite each other, but kept missing. One rolled onto its back, still playing the mouth game with the other. After a few minutes of such play, the one on its back suddenly ran off with its playmate in pursuit.

"Now they're playing chase," Kenzie said quietly.

From what Lory could see in the shadows, the wolves played the game much as the Lightfoot children had. Or was it the other way around? The two wolves frolicked in the yard, occasionally out of sight, and soon they were joined by others. The lead runner in chase bounded back through the yard, switching direction with an abruptness that suggested no prior thought. Suddenly all the players, chasers and runners alike, stopped, and Lory could see them tilting their heads as if listening to some far off sound. Nearly as one, they let out a chorus of howls.

Still conditioned by a culture that feared and hated wolves, Lory inhaled sharply, feeling his earlier terror wash over him.

Kenzie's smaller hand peeled the fingers of his one hand off the window sill. "It's all right, Lory. Howling is just how they talk."

Lory turned to her. For all her youth she sounded more wise than he could ever hope to be. "That's not what I learned growing up."

She smiled. "Your people fear us because they don't understand us."

"I don't fear you, Kenzie. It's the wolves I'm scared of."

"You can't fear one and not the other." She patted his hand. "If you learn to understand the wolf, you'll realize there's no reason to fear either of us." She looked out the window and smiled again.

Lory sighed, not quite understanding her words. How could one so young speak so cryptically? He looked back out the window to the wolves below. They stopped howling. As a group they turned and melted back into the woods. The last one turned briefly, looking over its shoulder toward the window. Lory froze, certain it could see him.

"She likes you, you know," Kenzie said softly.

Lory turned to her, alarmed. "The wolf?"

Kenzie grinned. "Kiana."

"She does?" He'd felt so stupid around her earlier, how could she possibly like him?

"You're not like the others." She quietly got to her feet.

"Which others?"

"Your people, Lory. You're not like the others we've met." She grinned impishly. "I've got to get back to bed before someone notices I'm not there and howls to the alphas."

Lory watched the girl walk silently to the curtain at the other end of the room. He turned and looked back out the window. There was no sign below that wolves had played there. He slowly got up and made his way back to his pad. He knew he wasn't as quiet as Kenzie had been, but he didn't want to wake the others who'd bedded down while he slept earlier. He snuggled back into his covers, warm and comfortable. But it was a long time before sleep came again.

* * *

133

Unfamiliar noises woke Lory. For a moment he forgot where he was, and he sat up with a start. The male Lightfoots were all up and about, preparing for the day. Remembering Lucas's words the day before, Lory hastened to follow their example. He had to scramble to catch up, but when Fang descended to the common room, Lory was not far behind.

Breakfast was evidently more informal than dinner, and Lory carefully copied the behaviors of those around him. He was half-way through his second roll with jam when he heard the approaching commotion of children.

"Lory, Lory!" Kenzie ran across the room to him. "Will you play with us?"

"You need to eat," he said, reaching out to ruffle her hair.

"Oooh, pettings," she said with a giggle. "Have I been good?"

"Of course you've been good." He continued to run his hand over her hair, since it had pleased her so much. "But now you need to eat."

"Will you play with us after?"

"We'll have to see," he tempered. He knew better than to make a promise to this one, she'd insist that he keep it. "I'm supposed to do some work for your father today."

She shook her head.

"What?"

"Not for him. It's for the pack," she announced cheerfully. "Everything's for the good of the pack."

"Teaching Lory pack philosophy, Kenzie?" Kiana asked, stepping behind the girl and placing both hands on her shoulders. She smiled when the girl looked up at her.

Lory met Kiana's fascinating eyes and smiled. These Lightfoots were quite aptly named. Any of them could sneak up on him and he wouldn't know they were there until they chose for him to. "Good morning, Kiana."

"And good morning to you, Lory. I trust you slept well?"

He nodded. Even if he hadn't, he never would have admitted it.

"Good." She looked around then. "I think Lucas is outside.

When you're ready, he'll show you what needs to be done."

"I'll help him," Fang said, speaking for the first time that morning. He looked up at his sister. "May as well learn something if I can."

Kiana smiled. "Thank you, Fang." She reached over and patted his head before turning away to check on Kenzie's breakfast progress.

Fang grinned, looking quite pleased with himself. His expression quickly changed when he noticed Lory watching him. "Trust me, even if you're a master builder you'll need help."

Lory nodded. "I was hoping someone would volunteer. Kiana made it sound like there was a lot to do."

Although he'd initially doubted Kiana's assessment of the work to be done, he soon realized she'd been correct. He also realized it would take more than a day or two to even get repairs underway. There was a very nice tool bench inside the barn, which turned out to be more of a massive storage shed since they kept no animals and didn't farm. Lory wondered how long it had been since anyone had used the tools kept there. Some well seasoned boards leaned against the far wall. Fang explained that they'd bought what they thought they might need during a trip into a village a year or so back, but so far no one had been sure where to start.

Lory assessed all the major damage first, then started Fang on cleaning up the rough edges of a hole in the roof of the barn. Once he was sure Fang was settled, he went to find Lucas.

"Mr. Lightfoot," he said, fidgeting as he approached the man from behind. "I need to talk to you about these repairs."

Lucas turned away from the children he'd been watching, and gestured for Lory to come closer. "Do you have enough tools, the right tools? Is there something else you need?"

Lory shook his head. "No, I think all the tools I need are there." It had surprised him to see the variety of tools in the barn, although they looked as though they were as old as the house. "It's just that there are so many things that really need to be done."

"We don't expect you to do everything, you know," Lucas said with an amused grin. "You're only one man, and even I know there's a lot to do."

Lory nodded. "Well that's just it. I could be here a month and not finish everything. And I really can't stay that long."

"Would it help if I sent a few others to help you?" Lucas asked. "You could supervise while they work. It'd be good for them to learn. We no longer have anyone in the forest trained to do these things."

Immensely relieved, Lory nodded again. "Things would move much faster, and I'd be happy to teach what I can while I'm here."

Lucas smiled. "Very well. I'll send you a few more."

Lory started back toward the barn.

"Oh, and Lory," Lucas called.

Lory abruptly stopped and turned, concerned he'd broken some rule. "Yes sir?"

"We don't expect you to fix everything before you leave."

* * *

Holding a nail with one hand, Lory grabbed the head of the hammer with the other. He unhooked the hammer from his belt and deftly flipped it, landing the handle in his palm. With two good strikes the nail was sunk. He gave it a few gentle taps to be sure it was all the way in. "It's important to sink the nail far enough that you won't scratch yourself on it later," he explained through the nails he held in his teeth. "And you want to be careful not to whack the piece you're nailing. Those dents will rot faster." He placed a second nail and tapped it into place as well. "Your aim'll improve, but don't be surprised if you hit your thumb a few times."

Fang groaned. He'd already hammered his fingers several times that morning and wasn't looking forward to more of it.

Lory glanced at the young man and smiled. "It might help to hit the nail lighter. It'll take a little longer but that doesn't matter." He gave Fang the hammer and left him to finish the repairs to the window frame. He'd put a number of the older Lightfoot children to work on one task or another, and it seemed to be going quite well. Supervising others was a change and it made him wish he would do it for a living. In his village, that didn't seem likely.

After a quick stop in the barn for tools, he returned to the roof to continue his patchwork. It was the most difficult and dangerous repair that needed to be done, and it wasn't something that could wait. Although Fang had done well enough clearing out the debris, bent nails, and rotten chunks of wood, he'd nearly fallen off the roof on his way back down. Not wanting to be responsible for someone else's injury, Lory relocated Fang to the ground and took over the roof himself.

He'd nearly finished his project when he paused, suddenly feeling as if someone were watching him. He looked up, and sitting across the apex from him was Kiana. Though startled, he was careful not to lean back and lose his balance.

She smiled, apparently pleased to have surprised him. "Hello."

"What are you doing up here?" he asked. He'd been intent on his work, but surely he should have heard her clambering up the ladder. "Don't you realize you could get hurt?"

"You're up here," she said.

"Yes, but I'm used to it," he said, quick to point out that detail. "Fang nearly fell this morning."

She nodded. "Is that why you're doing this?"

He nodded. "Makes the most sense."

"And what if you fall, Lory?"

"It wouldn't be the first time." He looked over the edge and shrugged. "And I'd probably break something."

She shook her head, then held up a dishtowel wrapped bundle. "You've been working hard, but you still need to eat."

"I'm almost done..."

She reached for the hammer and pulled it away, nearly tipping backward.

Lory grabbed her wrist, pulling her back toward the apex until she'd regained her balance. "Don't do that Kiana!" he snapped. "This is no place for playing around."

She nodded.

He let go of her wrist and let out a breath. "I'm sorry. I shouldn't have yelled at you like that." He hoped he hadn't offended her too much with his reprimand, but she'd scared him.

"That's okay. You're right." She handed him the bundle. "Since I knew you wouldn't come down to eat, I brought it up. I thought maybe you'd take a break then."

He nodded and crawled a little closer to the peak. The he turned over so he could sit while he ate. "I can't eat all this," he protested when he untied the corners of the towel.

Kiana climbed over the apex to sit next to him, on the side away from the edge of the roof. "That's because it's my lunch too." She snatched out a sandwich and began to eat.

* * *

By early evening, Lory was beginning to feel the effects of a hard day of work. He'd fretted the entire time Kiana was up on the roof, and had been utterly relieved once he saw her safely back on solid ground. He'd no sooner returned to earth when he was needed to help with a project two of her sisters had been working on. They both seemed to have a bit of natural talent for detail work, so he'd set them to repairing trim around the windows and doors.

He was just getting started on a new project of his own when he heard the shout.

"Runner coming through!"

A single wolf tore through the yard, just past where Lory was showing Fang how to make cedar shingles to replace those that had gone bad. He held his breath as the large gray canid passed by. He tried to force himself to relax. Kenzie and Kiana had told him over and over there was nothing to fear of wolves. They'd lived here forever, and must surely know better than he.

"Are you all right?" Fang asked after the wolf disappeared into the woods on the other side of the yard.

Lory nodded. "I will be."

Fang grunted. "They really won't hurt you."

"So I've heard," Lory said. "But until recently I'd been told something entirely different."

Fang grunted again. "The unknown should always be approached with caution, but for your people ignorance often breeds fear and superstition."

Lory met Fang's amber eyes. "I'm beginning to think you're right."

* * *

After dinner, Lory was once again called upon to play with the children. Although tired, he acquiesced deciding that it was probably impossible to say no to Kenzie. He didn't catch any of them that evening, and they played until Kiana called them in to bed.

She stood outside the door, waiting until every last one of them went in. Once they had, she closed the door and walked out into the yard where Lory still stood. "How are you doing?"

He shrugged. "I don't remember the last time I was this tired." He saw her smile and was glad he'd responded that way. He felt her fingers close around his.

"Walk with me, Lory." She started off away from the house.

His hand was like a tether and he would have followed her anywhere.

"Fang told me that you saw the runner today."

He nodded, forgetting that she might not see in the dark.

"Were you scared of him?"

Ashamed, but unable to lie, he nodded. "Yes," he whispered.

She stopped walking and reached for his other hand. "Can I tell you a story?"

"Yes," he whispered again.

"A long, long time ago, hundreds or even a thousand years ago, a small family made its way into the great forest. They were tired of the kings and rulers of their home and wanted a life where only the truly important things mattered.

"But the family knew nothing of living in the woods. They were frightened by the animals and the strange noises. They knew little of hunting and foraging in the forest. They were hungry and cold. They were miserable and began to think of going back to the horrible land they'd fled. Just as they were about to give up, a wolf came out from behind the trees. 'Don't be afraid,' she said. 'I mean you no harm.'

139

"The family was scared, nonetheless. 'What do you want,' they asked. 'We have little, but you can have it if you will spare our lives.' When they said that, the wolf laughed at them. She didn't want their things. What use would a wolf have for clothes or pans or silverware?"

Lory smiled at that irony.

Kiana continued. "When she was done laughing, she said, 'I will teach you what you need to know to live in the forest, but you must give me something in return.' Of course the family was confused. She'd refused their things, so what could they possibly give her in exchange? 'You must never forget that I did this for you,' she said. 'From this day on, our families are as the same. We will be as brothers and sisters, watching out for each other, protecting each other, and helping each other above all else.'

"The family had little choice if they wanted to stay in the forest, and they trusted the wolf more than they trusted the kings and rulers. She had been honest with them, where their own kind had not. Although they didn't really understand what the agreement would entail, they accepted the wolf's proposal. And to this day the descendants of those families still live in this forest and still abide by their agreements to each other."

After she finished the story, they stood in silence. Lory wasn't sure what to say, and he knew she was waiting for a response. "Were they the first of the Lightfoots?"

"Yes." There was a long moment before she continued. "And once they made the agreement with sister wolf, they were forever changed. She gave us many gifts, and we are grateful. Not afraid."

"I know I shouldn't be afraid Kiana, and I'm trying " he halted abruptly when he felt her fingers brush his lips.

"I appreciate your effort. And you're far more open-minded than most. I just want to help you understand more and fear less before you leave us." She took his other hand again. "Your time with us is short, Lory, and it's very important to me that we send you on your way with the truth. It happens sometimes that someone finds their way to us, and very few can find their way out again without our help. But most won't listen to the truth."

"I'm only one person. What good will it do if I understand and no one else does?"

She smiled, her teeth reflecting what little light there was. "It always starts with a single person, Lory. There can never be change of heart without the ideas and actions of one person. You can be that person. Or you can go back to your warped ideology, comfortable and familiar."

"But..."

"Your people have killed my people over this Lory," she said as sternly as he'd ever heard her speak.

He stared at her in horror. "I'm so sorry," he whispered, horrified. He was an intruder, and one of the enemy. She could have left him in the woods when he was lost. She and her family could have killed him in retaliation for what had happened to their people. "Fang said there was room in the forest for more packs," he said quickly. "Is that what he meant? Whole families have been killed because of this?"

"Yes."

He swallowed, suddenly feeling ill. He jerked his hands out of hers and turned away, shuddering.

Kiana walked around him and tried to pull his hands away from his face.

He stepped back but wouldn't let her hold his hands as he looked at her. "How can you even stand to be around me?" he demanded.

"You didn't do those things, Lory. I don't think you could." She took a step closer but didn't try to touch him.

"Why didn't someone tell me before?" Instead of telling him, they had welcomed him into their home and fed him. They let their children play with him.

"The signs were there Lory, you just didn't see them."

"But, you've been so nice to me. Everyone has."

"Your people have hurt us, but we've decided, all the packs have decided that it would be worse to actively attack your people. It would only justify the further slaughter of innocents. And we are not interested in battles." She sighed. "If we could show your people we mean no harm, perhaps they would be more accepting of us."

Lory shook his head. His village alone had never been known for tolerance. The strange and unusual were cast out as evil, and no explanation was permitted. "Maybe if you didn't advertise your beliefs "

"We are what we are, Lory," she snapped. "We owe the wolf everything, and unlike others who have made promises in the past, we can never go back on our word. Why should we hide who we are just because it makes you uncomfortable?"

"That's not what I meant," he said quickly, holding up his hands.

"It is, and you know it." She glared at him. "You have a sister, don't you?"

"Yes."

"Would you stand by and let someone kill her?"

"Of course not!"

"The wolf is my sister." She crossed her arms over her chest.

Lory stared at her as he tried to get his mind to accept everything she'd told him. A secret war had been raging for generations; it was entirely unnecessary, and this was the first he'd heard of it. The Lightfoots and others like them were willing to die to keep their word, while many of his own people kept a promise only as long as it was convenient. It wasn't right that those more honorable should be the ones to suffer most. On the whole, the Lightfoots seemed quite reasonable, so why should this one request, this one difference be so difficult to accept?

"I won't hurt your sister, Kiana," he said quietly. "And I'll try not to fear her."

* * *

Lory and Fang worked together most of the next day. It had taken both of them and two others to remove the heavy front door from its hinges. The door itself had been so well made it only needed a little clean up and a bit of staining to maintain it. The frame, however, had not endured the time and weather so well.

"Would you rather work on the door or the frame?" Lory asked.

142

"Which doesn't involve a hammer?" Fang's fingertips were red and his palms had identical rows of blisters across the first joint of each finger.

Lory smiled. "The door. You'll have to do some sanding, but it may be easier on your fingers than the pounding you gave them yesterday." The sand wouldn't exactly be gentle on his abused hands, but it would be a useful skill for him to learn.

When talking with Lucas at breakfast, they had decided he should leave the following morning. Lory's family would be worried, and he had a life to return to. Still feeling that he wasn't getting as much done as he ought, Lory continued to check on the progress of the other projects throughout the day. He'd lost track of time when Kiana came looking for him.

"Lory?"

He looked up from the door frame. "Hello." He hadn't seen her all day and had fretted that she was still angry with him about last night. Kenzie had brought his lunch today, and he was certain the beta female was avoiding him.

"Are you nearly done with that?"

He nodded. "I've replaced all the bad pieces." He ran his hands down both sides of the frame. He pulled the hammer from his belt and tapped a nail that wasn't quite sunk to his satisfaction. "I guess I'll just have to wait until Fang's done with the door, but this should be done."

"Would you walk with me?"

Lory stood up, looking at her again, almost as if for the first time. "Are you mad at me?"

She smiled and shook her head. "We don't stay angry long."

He sighed in relief. "I was sure you were ignoring me."

"I've been busy, same as you." She grinned up at him. "And there's something I want to show you."

"What is it?" he asked as he started to follow her.

"It's a surprise," she said, looking over her shoulder at him as she headed for the woods. "My father said you'd be leaving tomorrow," she said, once he'd caught up. "And I wanted to give you the chance to see this."

"Where've you been all day?"

"You'll know once we get where we're going," she answered.

Confused, Lory followed in silence. They'd been walking for some time when Kiana stopped and tilted her head as if to listen. Lory followed her example. For a moment he thought he heard a very soft squeaking. It wasn't like any bird he knew.

"Right over here." She walked a few paces and pushed aside the branches of a shrub. "See," she pointed to the ground at the base of the bush.

Lory stepped closer, looked and saw a small mound of gray fur, no bigger than a barn cat. As he watched it, it moved just a little, and he realized the little mound of fur had eyes. Pleased that he hadn't so much as flinched, he looked at Kiana. "Is that a wolf?"

She grinned in delight then bent to scoop up the pup. "He's just a baby, but yes, he is."

Lory held a tentative hand out and nearly stepped back when the nose brushed his fingers. It hadn't bitten Kiana. It wouldn't hurt him either. Besides, it was so little. "Won't its mother be upset that you moved him?"

She shook her head. "His mother's been missing for days." She kissed the stubby little muzzle. "A wolf doesn't leave her babies for that long unless she's hurt or dead. He's part of our pack now, unless she comes back."

She was clearly delighted with the puppy, so Lory reached out to touch it again. "His hair is so soft."

"He hasn't gotten his waterproof coat yet," she told him. "His fur will get coarser when that happens." She held out the puppy to him. "Want to hold him?"

He hesitated only a moment, before carefully taking the young wolf the way he'd seen her hold him. The wolf whimpered for a moment, but settled down when Lory caressed his head. Two days ago he never would have guessed he'd be holding a wolf, and he grinned.

"We should get back," Kiana said. "He'll be hungry, and the others have been waiting to see him."

Lory followed her back toward the house, stepping carefully as not to disturb his cargo. "How'd you know he was here?"

"We were told," she said offhandedly. "A pack-to-pack runner came through with the news and since we're the closest he's our responsibility."

"Will he be much trouble?"

"Oh no," she shook her head. "They never are."

"So you've done this before?"

She paused and looked at him. "Life in the forest is naturally difficult, but usually enough members of a pack survive to keep it going. They would usually be the ones to take care of such unfortunate babies." She petted the pup's head.

"So where are they?" he asked, almost certain he knew.

"They've been killed. His mother was probably shot." She turned and continued back to the house.

Lory looked carefully at the puppy before following her. He was so little and vulnerable. Nothing like the wolves he'd been taught to fear. He'd never considered the possibility that they had families and babies, very much like people did.

If anyone was surprised that Lory was carrying the pup when they returned to the house, they didn't mention it. However, Kenzie was quick to point out that he didn't appear to eager to turn the little animal over to anyone else.

* * *

The entire pack turned out to wish him on his way, and Lory was quite embarrassed by their effusive thanks for the work he'd done. Kenzie let him hold the pup, who was now called Wachay, one last time. The pup even licked Lory's face before being returned to Kenzie's waiting hands. She had apparently designated herself as his nursemaid, and Lory knew Wachay would receive the best possible care.

When he looked back over his shoulder, he could see the pack, still standing and waiting. He was pleased that Kiana had chosen, or been chosen, to lead him back out, but now that they were alone, he could think of nothing to say. Kiana seemed equally introspective, and they walked in near silence.

* * *

"Do you know where you are?" Kiana asked.

Lory looked around and nodded. They had walked for what felt close to two hours, maybe more. "I can find my way from here." They weren't far from the edge of the forest, and it wouldn't take him long to get home. "Are you sure you can make it back before dark?"

She smiled up at him. "I'll be fine, Lory. The forest is my home, remember? And it doesn't take long when I'm on my own."

He nodded, disappointed. She was entirely too independent, and he'd known that from the start. She didn't need to come home with him. "Thanks for everything."

She shrugged. "Let it never be said that a Lightfoot wouldn't lend a hand to a stranger who needed it."

He smiled. "You did that and more, you know. And I don't quite know what to say."

"Then say nothing Lory, and let the silence speak for itself." She took a step back. "Now you should go, time's wasting."

"Could I come back?"

"That's for you and the future to determine."

He sighed. He should have known he wouldn't get a straight answer out of her. She touched his hand and he met her amber eyes.

"If you're of good heart, and you truly want to come back, you'll be able to. That's all I can tell you."

Before he could change his mind, he bent quickly to kiss her cheek. He was surprised to feel her hand on the back of his neck. She pressed her cheek to his for a moment, then stepped back. For once she wasn't smiling, and he hoped she felt at least a little sad right now, because he certainly did.

He turned and walked a dozen paces before looking back over his shoulder. He froze. Where he had left Kiana, sat a nearly black wolf. She was not especially large, having a less stocky build than some he'd seen while visiting the Lightfoots. She watched him, with eyes so light a brown they appeared to be amber. Watching the wolf, he slowly continued on his path. After a few moments the wolf got to her feet, turned, and loped back toward home.